memory of Latasha Harlins (1975–1991)
and
dward Jae Song Lee (1973–1992)

...ss Cataloging-in-Publication Data

...ye / Marie G. Lee.

...this sequel to "Finding My Voice," Ellen Sung explores
...eative writing and in her Korean heritage during
...r at Harvard.
...7066–7
...ericans—Fiction.   2. Harvard University — Fiction.
...nd colleges — Fiction.   4. Prejudices — Fiction.
... Fiction.   6. Authorship — Fiction.]   I. Title.
...1994   93–26092
              CIP
              AC

...ited States of America

   7   6   5   4   3   2

To t

Sayin

MA

Copyright (

All rights re
to reproduc
Permissions
Avenue Sou

Library of Co

Lee, Marie G
  Saying goo
    p.   c
  Summary:
her interest ir
her freshman
    ISBN 0–395
  [1. Korean
3. Universitie
5. Friendship
PZ7.L5138Say

HOUGH

Printed in the U

VB   10   9

Acknowledgments

Writing a book is a lot like maintaining a friendship: it requires perseverance, it can have its ugly patches, but it is always ultimately fulfilling and worthwhile.

So, to friends: thanks lots to Mary Kim, who makes sure I get out and play once in awhile, to Dr. Dede Blake, who's always with me in spirit, and to the folks at the Asian American Writers' Workshop, especially Christina Chiu, Curtis Chin, and Bino Realuyo. I can never express enough thanks to Wendy Schmalz for her "motivational talks" and lunchtime companionship, and to Laura Hornik for her wisdom, friendship, and benevolent — but firm — editorial hand.

And, as always, thanks to my family and to Karl.

"We are caught in an inescapable network of mutuality. Whatever affects one directly affects us all indirectly."

— Dr. Martin Luther King, Jr.

Chapter One

"I CAN'T BELIEVE I ever thought of you as a friend!" Leecia screamed — the first time she'd ever raised her voice to me. "You are nothing but a liar!"

This happened on the same day that my best friend from home, Jessie, called to tell me that she'd read the short story I'd written about her and that she'd never, ever talk to me again.

*

Getting into Harvard, my parents told me, meant that I'd be set for life. I knew there had to be some reason for the rigid curfews, extra homework assignments, and despair I'd suffered through high school. My friends went to parties on weekends; I was the only one who ever had to stay in to do homework ("B's aren't good enough" was my father's favorite saying). I was the only one who sweated through pages and pages of labyrinthine college application forms, genuflected daily to the mailbox all through April, and eventually left for college via the local airport, not the bus station.

Not until leaving did I have the first inkling that perhaps not everything was going to be happily-ever-after. It hurt to say goodbye to my parents, my best friend Jessie, my old boyfriend Tomper, the town I'd lived my whole life in. I never knew anything could hurt so bad. In the summer it had been easy to say, "Yeah, I'm going to Harvard." Everyone said, "Great, at least *you'll* be getting out of this shitty little town," and I smugly agreed, never stopping to consider what it meant to go away to school in Cambridge, Massachusetts. I didn't know until it was too late that it meant leaving, it meant saying goodbye.

*

"Since there's so much traffic in the Yard, just drop us in front of the gates over there."

Michelle, practically leaning over the cabby's shoulder, points to where she wants him to go. We are nearing The Place, and the tree-lined streets suddenly become familiar to me. As I'm sitting there on the lumpy taxi seat, I'm transformed into a kid again, visiting her big sis at her college, Harvard.

Then I remember that I'm supposed to be going here, too. Not visiting anymore.

I can't do this, I think frantically as the taxi pulls up to the wrought iron gates that mark the entrance to Harvard Yard.

It's not too late. I could have the cabby pull a screeching U-turn and take me back to the airport so I can return to Mom and Father and all my friends in Arkin. I could do it. I could late-register at the University of Minnesota. From there I'd probably go to med school. Mom and Father would be just as proud of me, right?

In the meantime, Michelle pays the fare by apportioning a precise collection of bills, quarters, dimes, and nickels. The driver counts the money, then shoves it into the cash box with neither a grumble nor a thank-you. As usual, Michelle has been exactly correct but not generous.

The next thing I know, she and I are on the curb with my assortment of suitcases and boxes, and the cabby has driven off.

"Here you are at Harvard," Michelle says, as if I should be pleased.

"I know," I say, gripping the handles of my suitcases. I can feel my palms sweat. Back in Minnesota, the dead chill of fall was nipping at the edges of the weather. Here, it's as hot and humid as if it were still summer.

We pass through the gates into stately Harvard Yard. In the middle of it is a statue of John Harvard sitting on a concrete pedestal that proclaims JOHN HARVARD, FOUNDER, 1638 — the statue of the three lies, I learned on my campus tour, since the college was founded not by John Harvard but by the General Court of the Massachusetts Bay Colony in 1636, and the likeness isn't even of John Harvard but of some random good-looking Harvard student of yore.

My academic career is probably starting on three lies, too: I'm not smart, I don't particularly want to go here (despite what I told my interviewer), and I'd rather hang out with my homespun friends from Arkin any day.

"Ellen, Weld is this way," Michelle says, motioning toward a vague corner of the Yard. I am suddenly grateful that she cut short her summer internship in New York to bring me to campus. I assured her I could do it on my own:

"I'm an adult, there's no need to stop your work." But she insisted, and now I'm glad.

We struggle on, making our way through broken threads of families. People are carting around stuffed animals, clothes, computers; overloaded Volvo station wagons nose their way past us. Ahead of us, two girls shout with surprise then embrace. How do they know each other? Except for Michelle, I know no one. Even my roommate, Leecia Thomas, is just a name from my WELCOME NEW STUDENTS packet.

I pause to watch all the commotion happening around me. Does anybody know that I'm Ellen Joyce Sung, a premed, inhabitant of Weld? Does anybody care?

"Come on, Ellen!" Michelle's voice, yards ahead of me, begins to boil with impatience. Guiltily, I scramble to follow her.

"This is it," she says finally, stopping in front of a red-brick building the color of dried blood. This one is conspicuously located in the very center of the Yard. The front door is propped open with a cement block. "Which room did you say you're in?"

"12C."

Michelle starts up the stairs that lead from the door. I follow, but my load seems to have grown heavier. I hoist the suitcases up a few steps, climb after them, hoist, rest.

"You okay with that?" A black-haired boy in a baseball cap and a Corona Beer tank top is on the stairs looking down at me.

"Oh, I'm fine," I say quickly. Sweat is beginning to trickle down my neck. To show him, I mightily heave the suitcases up another few steps. One of them misses and begins to topple back down on me. The boy moves quickly and catches it.

"Where to?" he says. His eyes are black and glittery, like a seal's. He grips the handles of both suitcases, and the muscles in his arms stand out in relief against his skin. I point to Michelle's quickly retreating back.

The boy practically floats up the stairs. By the time I get up there, the bags have been neatly deposited in front of Michelle, who has a scowl on her face. "We can manage by ourselves, thank you," she says. Her voice snaps like a whip on the *thank you*.

The boy good-naturedly waves before returning down the stairs. My self-reliant sister hates accepting help, especially from men — she thinks they're always scamming for women. But this guy was obviously just trying to be nice. And he's Oriental, like us — you'd think that would count for something.

"Who was *That*?" Michelle says, somewhat crankily, as I open the door with a key that says DO NOT DUPLICATE.

"Darned if I know," I say. The locks, I notice, are Yale locks. I thought Harvard hated Yale.

The door swings open, and I'm not sure what I expect, but I'm surprised nonetheless. Inside is what has been advertised as our "suite." Embassy Suites it's not: a common room with bare, skeletal bookshelves, a tiny bedroom, a bathroom with two sinks, an industrial stomp-to-flush toilet, a shower.

I'm supposed to be living here?

"Is this what your freshman room was like?" I ask

Michelle uneasily. Somehow, I remember hers as being better.

"It was just like this," she says. "Except that it was a five-person suite in Matthews — you must remember it. Jenny and I lived in that gross and drafty room."

I am going to spend the next year living in a matchbox, and with another person. Is this some kind of social experiment? In a lab, rats would probably be driven to chew off each other's ears. I don't even know how well I could live in here with Jessie, and we like — liked — to do everything together.

Michelle, however, sees nothing amiss, and she moves with military determination into the tiny bedroom. I follow. The room is lined on two sides with bare, narrow beds that look like they would be right at home in a prison or a mental hospital. Some interior decorator has also managed to shove two desks in here, leaving only a sliver of space to slither through.

Michelle rips open a suitcase and begins hanging my clothes. I work on very gently unpacking my plastic cow clock. Jessie gave it to me a few years ago as a joke, but now I think of it so fondly as one of the last links to my old life. For years this clock was the first thing I saw in the morning, the last thing I saw at night — back when I had my own room, back when I was a student at Arkin High.

"That thing is so ugly, Ellen," Michelle remarks, beginning to hang up sweaters, categorized by color.

"Thanks," I say, patting it as if it were a real Holstein.

"Hello? Anybody home?" A voice from the hallway. I venture out of the bedroom. In the doorway is a pretty girl with a garment bag slung over her shoulder. Her eyes are a dark chocolate brown, almost as dark as mine.

"Is this 12C?" she asks.

"Hi," I say. "It is."

"Great." The girl grins at me, then turns and calls over her shoulder, "This is it, guys! Heave ho!"

In the twinkling of an eye, the girl, her parents, one grandma, and a little brother and sister pile into the room along with all the girl's stuff: three suitcases, milk crates full of shoes, computer and printer, popcorn popper, lamps, Sony Watchman, garment bags, stereo/CD player, books, a poster.

"You must be Ellen," the girl says, her eyes dancing.

"You must be Leecia," I say. Leecia, my new roommate. I find I'm holding my breath. I try to let it out quietly.

Leecia introduces me to her family, and I introduce them to Michelle.

Then we all stare at one another.

Leecia's father speaks first. "We have a long drive back to Baltimore, honey," he says. "We'd better start unpacking."

"Sure, Dad," Leecia says obligingly. Then she turns and secretly slides me a grin. I find myself smiling back.

*

When I return from dinner with Michelle, Leecia is sitting cozily in the common room reading a book. She has wire-rimmed granny glasses perched on her nose.

"Did you have a nice dinner?" she asks.

"Uh-huh," I say, feeling vaguely uneasy, like nervous company. The furniture looks so unfamiliar, so uncomfortable.

"I hope you don't mind, I had my dad put up the poster since he had the hammer with him," she says, motioning to a framed print of ballet shoes on the wall. "But we can take it down easily enough."

"Oh no, it looks nice," I say. "Makes the place look homey."

Actually, it's Leecia who looks homey, sitting around all comfortable, as if she's always lived here. I feel like a caged gerbil in this room.

"Want some tea?" Leecia asks. "I have regular and herbal."

Tea sounds wonderful. "Sure," I say. "Herbal, please."

Leecia gets out her electric kettle, and soon enough I have a warm mug nestled in my hands. The tea has a small floating pillow in it that's charmingly pungent and redolent of apple pie.

"It's apple cinnamon," Leecia says, tucking her bare feet under her like a cat.

I finally sit down. Surrounded by the warm, familiar scent of cinnamon, I feel as though I might be starting to relax, just a tiny bit.

"So I can't believe they put the two of us together," Leecia says, just like that.

"Excuse me?" I say, sputtering a bit on the hot tea.

"They put an Asian American woman and an African American woman at the same address," she says. "You'd think they'd want to use us to spice up the diversity of some of the other housing groups."

"Oh, is there supposed to be a minority in every housing group?" I say, noting how Leecia used "Asian American" when referring to me, not "Oriental," as people in Arkin do.

"Ideally there would be — it's the whole diversity thing," Leecia says, nodding her head. "Multiculturalism is big right now. Even Harvard wants to make sure white students learn a little about exotic cultures while they're here."

"Right," I say, although I have also never personally known a black person. Leecia seems so sophisticated — I'm dying to know more about her.

"Do you have your high school yearbook here?" I ask.

"I do," Leecia says. She runs into the bedroom and returns with a blue leather-bound book in her hand. *The Pot Purri*, it says in silver letters on the cover. On the the inside it says Andover.

"It's a prep school in Massachusetts," she explains.

"But I thought you were from Baltimore."

"I am. It's a boarding school."

Andover, if it's anything like it looks in the book, is beautiful: green woods all around, a huge playing field, red-brick school buildings — the Harvard kind of look.

"Wow," I say. "People in prep school really do dress preppy." A lot of the boys are wearing button-down Oxford shirts and khakis; the girls are in sweaters and skirts. In my yearbook, the regular uniform is a Guns 'n' Roses T-shirt, preferably ripped.

Leecia doesn't seem very preppy, however. Right now she's wearing a funky black leotard top paired with faded and slightly ripped Levis.

I pass a picture that has tiny hearts drawn all over it. Ray Stevens, it says. Leecia isn't *too* different from me: in my yearbook, Jessie drew hearts with arrows through the pictures of Tomper and of her boyfriend, Mike.

"Your boyfriend, Leecia?" I ask.

"Oh, he was just a puppy-love sort of thing," she replies. "And anyway, people at Andover didn't really date too much, in a formal sense. Girls and guys lived in separate dorms, and there were hardly any opportunities to get together outside of class."

I dig out my Arkin *Taconite*. It sits next to my favorite book, *Stories from Above and Below,* a collection of short stories by Marianne Stoeller. My English teacher, Mrs. Klatsen, introduced me to Stoeller's writing last year.

"This is mine," I say, handing the yearbook to Leecia. It's kind of embarrassing that the book is falling apart already, pages breaking loose from the cheap glue binding. But Leecia looks at it carefully. She even stops to see what Jessie has written: "Ellen, we'll always be best friends, forever."

I wonder what Leecia would think of me if she knew how much I'm already pining away for my high school days. I still can't believe that I won't be going back to Arkin High tomorrow, or perhaps next week. I wish I could be more like Leecia — grown up, ready to get on to the next stage of life.

While Leecia is in the bathroom getting ready for bed, I impulsively run back to my yearbook and flip through it. In the sports section there's a picture of me, mid-flip at a gymnastics meet. Tomper and Mike are in the varsity hockey photo. Even in the grainy black-and-white reproduction I can see Tomper's clear blue eyes looking out at me.

I hear water running in the bathroom. A splash, a sneeze.

I miss Tomper. I miss Jessie. I miss Arkin. I admit it. But

even if I went back, it wouldn't be like it was. Tomper is gone — boot camp in North Carolina. We aren't in high school anymore.

I look through the *Taconite* again. In the miscellaneous pictures at the end there's a slightly off-center photo of Jessie giving me a piggyback ride.

The bathroom door opens. I shove the yearbook back into its place on the shelf.

When both Leecia's and my nightly rituals are done, we climb into our respective beds.

"Ready?" Leecia says, her hand poised over the light switch.

"Ready," I say.

In the dark, I am a buzzing bundle of nerves. What if I breathe too loud and disturb her? Heaven knows whether I snore or drool or sleepwalk. I have never before slept in a room with someone I didn't know.

As I am thinking all these things, I suddenly slip, as if off a steep cliff, into an exhausted sleep.

Chapter Two

WHEN I OPEN my eyes the next morning, nothing I expect to see is there: no yellow wallpaper, no daisy print curtains, no sounds of Mom clinking breakfast dishes downstairs.

Leecia, however, is awake and cheerful, and after quick showers we make our way over to the Union, the freshman cafeteria, for breakfast.

In the dark Union building, we walk past ominously bubbling vats of oatmeal to the cold cereal dispensers. I feel a sudden surge of freedom as I load up my tray with Sugar Smacks; sugared cereals are forbidden in the Sung household. Leecia chooses Shredded Wheat, plain and sensible.

"We have a busy schedule today," Leecia announces, looking at the fancy leather organizer she keeps with her. From the wall, a creepy oil-painted portrait of Teddy Roosevelt seems to be looking with her. "At eleven-thirty we meet our proctor and then have a welcoming picnic on the lawn. At three we get to meet the president, and at eight is an optional ice cream social. I suppose by the end of this, all of us freshpeople will be one big happy family."

"One big happy family," I echo, noticing that the Sugar Smacks have made my milk almost inedibly sweet.

"Hey, girl!" Someone with lots of long, skinny braids has her hand on Leecia's shoulder.

"Monica!" Leecia says, hugging her. "I was wondering when I'd run into you."

Wow, I think. Leecia knows someone here.

"This is my roommate, Ellen," Leecia says.

"Nice to meet you," Monica says to me, extending her hand.

"Monica and I went to elementary school and junior high together," Leecia explains.

"I've got to go, Lee-Cee," Monica says. "But want to do the ice cream social tonight?"

"Sure," Leecia says. "Come pick me up — Weld, 12C."

What should *I* do tonight, now that Leecia has another friend? I could always go hang out with Michelle, I suppose.

Some kind of missile lands in my cereal bowl, spraying sticky milk all over the place.

"What the — " says Leecia, looking around.

Some guys, howling with laughter, are hurling butter pats at the Union's high ceiling. Looking up, I see that there *are* some old yellow pats successfully stuck up there, but these guys don't seem to care that their attempts are landing in other people's cereal bowls.

"What a bunch of immature jerks," Leecia says, handing me some napkins. "Who let them in?"

~~At least it's an excuse for me to get rid of my sugary milk,~~ I decide.

*

A little before noon, Leecia and I gather with the thirty or so other residents of Weld in front of the dorm, where we meet our proctor. Leecia informs me that a proctor is someone who's paid to live with us and help orient us. He is thin and tall, with out-of-control hair and a huge Adam's apple that's covered with stubble.

"How do you know all this, Leecia?" I ask her. "Is there some student handbook I missed?"

"No, honey," she says, leaning familiarly on my shoulder and laughing. "My high school was Harvard training camp from day one. We were always talking about what it would be like to go here, we'd come here on weekends, and people who ended up going to Harvard were always coming back to Andover to give us the scoop on things."

"I see," I say.

"Hello, I'm Irwin Stone, your proctor," says the man. His eyes are sparkling with enthusiasm. Then he starts to cough violently; he must have something stuck in his throat. A guy in front of me, whose shoulders are so broad I can barely see past them, starts to snicker rudely. I glare at his back. Poor Irwin must be nervous.

"As I [cough] said, I'm Irwin and I'd to, I'm . . ." Irwin is struggling for self-control. He takes off his glasses to wipe the tears out of his eyes. "I'd like to welcome you all to Harvard," he finally spits out.

Irwin goes on to tell us that he graduated from Harvard three years ago, and now he's getting his Ph.D. in chemistry. He tells us he'll be living on the first floor with his wife, Ann Marie, and that we should come see him if we have any problems, academic or otherwise. His door is always open, he says.

"And now, do you have any questions for me?" he asks expectantly.

There is silence. Some of the guys begin to edge toward the picnic lunch. Irwin surveys us all disappointedly.

When we are officially set loose, people lunge at the food in earnest. I'm not in any big hurry, and neither is Leecia, so we watch the others scramble toward the mounds of waxed paper.

Out of the corner of my eye, I spot the black-haired boy who helped me with my baggage yesterday. He's looking my way, smiling and waving slightly. I turn to see who he's waving at, but I don't see anyone.

Leecia and I end up eating tepid sandwiches and potato chips with some other girls from our dorm: one's from San Francisco, the other's from Ohio. We don't talk a whole lot; after "Where're you from?" the conversation sort of dies down. I've noticed that the heckler and some other beefy guys have formed their own little group; they are guffawing and stuffing sandwiches down their gullets.

It's interesting to me the way guys bond so quickly. Often, their relationships seem to be based merely on the ability to discuss girls, sports, and beer. Female friendships, in contrast, are always so wary, so *serious*, right from the beginning. I guess I can't quite figure out why I'm willing to pour out my life to some girlfriends and can't get past hello with others.

Still, I'm not envious of guys. I like to have things in common with my friends besides each of us knowing the batting average of every player on the Minnesota Twins.

Out of curiosity, I look around to see who the black-haired boy is hanging around with, but he's nowhere to be seen.

*

"Hel-lo!" says Monica as she comes into our suite. "Ice cream time!"

Leecia puts on her shoes. "Ready to go?"

I look up to see that she's addressing me.

"Ready to go, Ellen?" she says.

I had resigned myself to spending the night alone, maybe going over the course catalog. I'm sure Monica wants to spend some time catching up with Leecia.

"Um, I think I'll stay in," I say. "I'm a little tired."

"Oh, no — are you that tired?" Leecia says. "It'd be fun if you came."

Something in her voice tells me she really means it. She wants me to come. Something joyful rises inside me.

"You twisted my arm," I say, jumping up.

Chapter Three

"Are we ready for classes or what?" Leecia says when we return from our library tour. There are more than thirteen million books in Harvard's hundred or so libraries, and we have supposedly just learned how to find them all.

"Speaking of classes," I say, "I'm supposed to go over to Michelle's about now because she's helping me choose mine."

"Must be nice having an upper-class sister tell you all the good classes to take," Leecia remarks half teasingly.

"She knows all the good *premed* classes," I remind her. Leecia told me she can't stand the sight of blood. "All the good bloody ones."

"Get out of here," Leecia says, playfully pushing me toward the door.

On my way out, I remember to grab my thick red *Courses of Instruction* book. It's not as if I didn't try to figure out my classes myself. I went through the catalog for two hours last night. But the science classes come in these bizarre sequences: for example, you have to take half of course B or all of X if you want to get into C, when there's no indication that you really need C in the first place. So how do you decide which courses are for the premeds and which are for the hard-core science types, the pre-Irwins?

I did speak with Irwin, too. I thought he might have some insights into chemistry classes. However, he just kept saying over and over, "This is Harvard, all the courses are good."

"But can you recommend a specific chemistry course or a good professor?" I insisted. "Out of all the sciences, I like chem the least, so can you suggest a good straightforward course to fulfill my premed requirements?"

"Really, you can't go wrong whichever course you take," he said, scratching his nose thoughtfully.

I paused for a moment, then I repeated myself, louder.

"Aaah." Irwin said something different, finally. Then he admitted that he couldn't remember much from his undergrad days, at least not enough to advise me. I couldn't help wondering what people with Ph.D.'s in chemistry do, other than become mad scientists.

I *did* make one wonderful discovery in my course search: my all-time favorite writer, Marianne Stoeller, is actually teaching a course here. I was so excited that I yelped out loud, startling Leecia, who was also reading the catalog.

Leecia, of course, wanted to know what was up, and I actually told her about the course, told her that I was interested in writing. It was slightly freaky, considering that I've hidden this fact of my life from everyone who's close to me — my parents, Michelle, Jessie — and here I go suddenly and very naturally revealing the secret to someone I have known for about a week.

But maybe *because* Leecia doesn't know me very well — that I've never written a whole story before, that since I was twelve, I've told everyone I was going to be a doctor — she didn't act like I was crazy but instead said to "go for it."

*

"Hi there," I say to Michelle as I walk into her room. She is staring intently at a plastic model of a molecular structure. She snaps out of her stare, carefully sets the model back into its appointed place on the shelf, and looks at me.

"Ready?" she says. I nod, proffering my catalog.

She opens the book familiarly and puts her finger on a class. "You need to take Bio 1."

"Righto," I say, copying the course number onto my registration sheet.

"Then you need to take inorganic chemistry, which is the prerequisite for orgo, the really tough one."

"Okey-dokey," I say.

"You have to take this math course," she says, pointing to something that looks suspiciously like calculus.

I write it down.

"For your fourth course, I'd suggest you fill up one of your core requirements. Let me try to find you a good humanities gut."

"Actually, Michelle," I cut in, "I was thinking of taking that course on short stories."

"Is that a core course?" Michelle says, flipping to the English section. "Literature?"

"Um, no." My stomach rumbles nervously. "It's a writing course."

Michelle slowly closes the book, her finger marking the page.

"A writing course?" she says. "Ellen, doctors don't need to take courses in writing."

"I'm interested in writing," I say with a gulp.

"You are?" she says, looking at me as if I'm under the influence of some virus that affects your brain. "I've never known you to be interested in writing."

I shrug. "I am. I just didn't go around advertising it."

"Can't you just do it on your own? Why waste a whole class on it?"

"The teacher, Marianne Stoeller, is really distinguished," I say. How can I explain to Michelle, who thinks fiction is useless because "it's all made up," that I've read Marianne Stoeller's stories so many times I almost feel that I know her, that I could trust her with the stories I want to tell?

"I've never heard of her," Michelle says.

"You're not going to hear about her in the *Lancet*," I tell her, and then I add, "There've been a lot of doctors who write, including Harvard people, like Perri Klass and Ethan Canin."

"That's not a *lot* of doctors by anyone's count," Michelle says. "Ellen, if I were you, I'd take either Survey of Western Philosophical Thought or this American history gut. Your science classes are going to take up a lot of time, so you should take a course that's easy and that you can get a good grade in."

Grades. That's right. I'm supposed to get good grades here. I keep thinking that after working so hard in high school, I should get a break. In high school, the refrain was always "You need good grades to get into Harvard." Now it's "You need good grades to get into medical school." I don't think the cycle even stops there; I think I am growing up.

"So what'll it be?" Michelle says.

I sit up, so I can at least *look* more confident. I've learned a lot about life, especially in the past year, and I've come to the conclusion that I have to stand up for myself, trust my own instincts. It's very possible that I'll be a dud in this class, but I have to find out if I can write. At the very least, I have to give it the old college try.

My doubts attach themselves like tiny sinkers to my stomach, but I write Short Stories 45A in the fourth blank.

"But I do appreciate your advice," I say to Michelle.

"It's your life," Michelle says, shaking her head.

*

"I found a course for you," Leecia says when I return.

"What is it?"

"Asian American literature," she says, reading from her copy of the catalog. " 'A course that explores the seminal works of Chinese American, Japanese American, Filipino American, and Korean American authors.' "

"Hm," I say. I *had* actually seen that course in the catalog, but it hadn't registered with me at all. When I think of literature I like to read, I think of Mark Twain or Flannery O'Connor or Marianne Stoeller. I was never that into *The Joy Luck Club*.

"Don't you think the course sounds great?"

"That's really sweet of you, to look out for courses for me," I say. "But I only get one elective as a premed, so

I'm going to take the short stories class I told you about."

"But if you're interested in writing, don't you first want to get acquainted with the literature?"

"The literature?" I say.

"Asian American literature," Leecia says, as if it's obvious. "You're Asian, so doesn't it make sense to study those works?"

"I guess," I say noncommittally. Does that make me some kind of weirdo — being Asian but not especially interested in reading Asian authors? Leecia looks a little disappointed, but what can I do?

"So what courses are *you* taking?" I say to change the subject.

"I have five that I'm interested in," she says, perking up. "African American history, African American women writers, political science, psychology, and an intro sociology class. I'm going to go to them all and then decide."

"Sounds good," I say. I head to the bedroom, pull out *Stories from Above and Below,* and begin reading in the quasi-privacy of the bedroom.

I've read these stories countless times before, but I don't mind doing it again. Something about Stoeller's words, even when I know they're coming, strikes me at exactly the right time. In my favorite story, "Roseland," I can feel the heady sensation of taking a lover, even though I've never had one in my life. I've had a boyfriend, but not a lover. And there is a difference.

> Every time I looked up, I saw him staring at me,
> his gaze seemingly fixed as if he were put on earth

only to look at me. As our eyes kept meeting, matching look for look, I wondered, did he think the same of me?

There was nothing furtive in our glances.

*

When I show my list of classes to my assigned premed adviser, she looks it over and signs it, just like that. No comments, good or bad, on my science class picks, no funny look about the short stories class. Professor Mertz merely hands my registration sheet back to me and I leave her office, passing a line of her other premed advisees. Maybe someone should buy her an auto-pen. I'm assuming she would have said something if my course choices had been totally unacceptable — say, four music theory courses. But I'm realizing now how truly on my own I am here: all the freedom to choose, but with responsibility for the consequences.

Chapter Four

ORIENTATION HERE largely means that we have to attend a lot of workshops. The most recent one was called "Communication and Group Dynamics Skills," which was a fancy way to label an attempt to teach us how to live harmoniously in a dorm with a bunch of strangers.

This workshop, however, didn't tell us a thing about how to get along with people in Weld. Case in point: Leecia and I have discovered that we have the misfortune of being located across the hall from two of the beefy guys — football players, we've learned. I don't have anything against football players — Tomper was one, as a matter of fact — but these particular guys assume that everyone will think whatever they do is wonderful because they play football for Harvard. They definitely look like butter-pat throwers.

The other night they spent the time from midnight to one trying to synchronize the Remainders' "Love Sux" playing on a CD player in their room with a tape in a boom box out in the hall. They thought they were being adorable. Leecia and I and everyone else in the hall never asked them to turn it down.

And why do we put up with this? For me, it's a simple lack of guts. I'd rather wear earplugs when I'm studying and sleeping than have to confront these guys. I keep hoping that one day they'll have some sort of revelation and they'll behave themselves.

Leecia, though, actually goes out of her way to be cordial to them. "I want to try to offset my preformed prejudices against them," is her explanation.

"That's very considerate of you," I remark. "Although they don't seem to be very considerate back."

"We'll give it a little time. The smarter side sometimes has to be the one to give; otherwise, no one gets anywhere."

But for now, neither of our approaches has seemed to work. The Neanderthals, as we affectionately (and secretly) call them, have been noisy, messy, and rude.

The night before classes start, in fact, the guys decide it's a good time for a party. At midnight, heavy metal music worms into my ears, through my earplugs.

"Maybe this will help," Leecia says, rising from bed to pull out her environments CD, a collection of nature sounds. She pops it in her player. A babbling brook warbles out.

The sounds of water and wind do help to some degree, but every so often I am shocked awake by a screech of laughter, a crash, a blast of music. I can hear Leecia tossing late into the night.

The next morning we both feel tired and horrible. We open the door to go to breakfast and can't believe what we see. Shards of broken glass, beer bottles, and crinkled plastic cups are scattered everywhere. A hall trash can has been overturned, and in front of our door, the broken neck of a beer bottle leers — not to mention the vomit/old beer/ garbage smell greeting our morning-sensitive noses.

Our first day of class.

"Those pigs!" Leecia fumes. She disappears back into the suite and returns with a broom and dustpan. Meticulously, she sweeps up enough to clear a safe path for us. Then, to my surprise, she walks over to the guys' door and knocks on it — loudly. A second later, she pounds even harder.

The door opens, and the forms of two huge, half-naked guys fill the frame. I gulp.

"What the *fuck* do you want?" says one, his hand tightening on the knob.

Leecia sighs melodramatically.

"I do believe this is yours," she says, dumping the dustpan full of broken glass, trash, and old cups onto the floor of their room.

Two mouths — three if you count mine — are forced into tight, round O's.

Leecia returns the cleaning equipment.

"Ready, Ellen?" she says to me.

I follow her, still speechless. The guys' door closes gently behind us.

"Leecia," I say as we get into the cold cereal line, "those guys are going to strangle us."

"Not if they know what's good for them," Leecia says. "Look, we tried being nice. Now we have to let them know that we aren't going to be pushovers as neighbors, right?"

"Uh, right," I say, admiration for Leecia mixed in with my fear of what those guys are going to do to us. I'm glad Leecia and I have classes all day.

*

· 26 ·

The chemistry professor hardly says hello to us before he starts scrawling formulas on the board. When one of the many boards becomes filled, a whirring noise begins, and the board just disappears into a slot on the platform.

I never would have thought so many students would want to be doctors. The class is huge, a capacity crowd occupying the rows of seats that rise in tiers from the professor's platform. It's kind of like taking a class in a stadium.

I take notes furiously, and am just a little lost at the end of my first class.

My math class in the afternoon is also large, and I recognize some of the people from chem.

The funny thing is that there is a sea of Asians in both math and chem. There are a lot of Asians at Harvard in general, but this is my first experience of being surrounded by them in class.

Of course, I knew things were going to be different here. In Arkin, if you peered into any classroom on a given day, you would see what looked like a Mueslix ad: rows and rows of blond perfection strained from the genes of the Finns, Swedes, and Norwegians who settled in Arkin years ago. Even Joey Aiello, the sole Italian kid in my class, complained about feeling weird because of his dark hair. You can imagine how I stuck out.

So now I'm here with people who look like me, and it's a disappointingly big so-what. Somehow, I thought I'd feel magically connected, more confident, whatever.

I guess I don't even know myself exactly what it means to be Asian/Korean American. Am I *really* Korean if I don't speak the language? When the classes ended, I noticed that some of the people who looked really American — Gap clothes, backpacks, etc. — started talking in some singsong language that I guessed was Chinese, possibly Korean. They had an ease about them, as if they were all born into the same family, leaving me to feel like a bewildered outsider.

I wonder if Michelle was any more prepared when she first came here. I know she doesn't think of herself in terms of Korea at all. "I'm Michelle, that's it" is her favorite saying. If pressed to reveal her nationality, she'll reply, "American." And while she considers "Asian American" a more politically correct label than "Oriental," she thinks actually going around calling yourself Asian American or Korean American is dumb. "Then we should be calling people Polish American or European American or whatever."

I mull this over for a second, then pack up my stuff to head to the library. It's the first day of classes, and I already have work to do. In a way that's good, because there's a certain familiarity in it. Studying is one thing I know I can do.

*

Returning to the dorm with Leecia after dinner, my knees grow weak when I see that our neighbors are home, door open.

I slink by first, trying to get to our door as fast as possible. But Leecia, to my disbelief, merely walks unhurriedly past their door, calling, "Hi guys!" as she passes.

Then I hear, "Hi, Leecia, hi, Ellen" — as respectful as can be.

We shut our door. Ashamed, I try to straighten out of my cowardly posture.

Leecia has spine. She won't let people push her around, and even those thickheaded football players realize it.

"Leecia," I say, "okay, I'm a coward, but I'm sure glad you put your foot down."

"You're not a coward," Leecia replies, making a face.

"I am," I say. "I was planning to let them run over me all year. At best I'd secretly call Security or do something really effective like siccing Irwin on them."

"You have your way of handling it and I have mine," she says. "I really didn't do anything — I just made them a little more mindful that there are other people who live in this dorm. I learned how to do it during my prep school days."

I like Leecia. I'm comfortable around her, I suddenly realize. We've crossed that line, gone from being strangers to being friends, and I like that feeling.

"I'm glad you're my roommate," I say.

Leecia turns, smiling a surprised, pleased smile.

"I'm glad you're mine, Ellen," she says.

Chapter Five

Marianne Stoeller, my short story teacher, rides a breeze into class. She wears loose, flowing clothes; a lilac-colored scarf at her neck flutters as she arrives. She is delicate and has bright eyes. She reminds me of the Emily Dickinson poem "I am small, like a wren."

Because the writing classes are supposed to be kept small, ours has only about fifteen people in it. We all sit at a round table. I try to figure out who looks the most writerly. The woman in the ripped jeans? The guy wearing the black turtleneck? The woman in the mismatched clothes and purple Birkenstock sandals? I'm in a T-shirt and khakis — depressingly pedestrian.

"Writing short stories is a lot like gardening," Marianne Stoeller says to us. "It takes a lot of time, a lot of care. But if done right, you'll produce works that will surprise you. I'm not saying that everyone here will get stories published, but you'll all learn to craft a story in your own voice."

Published? I'm just trying to get up the courage to commit a story to paper.

She hands out the syllabus, and I see we'll be using books like *The Art of the Tale* and other short story collections. To my disappointment, though, I see that we aren't going to be reading anything of hers.

Our first class is short, and I toy with the idea of asking Marianne Stoeller if we'll ever be reading any of her works. However, the girl with the ripped jeans reaches her first and begins talking quickly, intently. As I pass, I hear her say something about her "story that was published in. . . ."

This girl has already been published!

Michelle is probably right, I think in a sudden panic. *I'm nuts to take this class if people in here have already been published.* Thank goodness they provide us with a "shopping period," when it's supposed to be easy to drop and add classes. I could enroll in philosophy, no sweat. All I need to do is fill out a form at the registrar's.

I walk out the door and head to the registrar's office. The breeze is refreshingly cool; it's beginning to smell of dried leaves and loam. Everything is changing. I pick up a drop/add form.

*

That night as I wash up before bed, my soapy fingers run over the unevenness on the side of my face. I am sort of surprised that no one here has seemed to notice these ridges — incompletely healed skin that was once torn by the edges of a broken bottle. Once ravaged, I'm realizing, the skin always remembers. Boy, does it remember.

Jessie was there when it happened. She was always trying to help me, encouraging me to speak my mind. None of us dreamed that Marsha Randall would go after my face with a bottle.

But I learned from it, right? I learned that things won't start to happen unless I stand up for myself. If I live my life in fear of being called a racist name, or anything, no one will be to blame except myself.

What would Jessie think, I wonder, about my dropping a class I dearly want to take just because I'm scared? How can I abandon something without trying it?

I carefully place the drop/add form in the wastebasket, and I lie down to sleep with a sigh.

*

One of our last freshman-week rites is to attend an activity fair, where we are supposed to learn about extracurricular activities at Harvard.

"We must figure out what to do with all our *copious* free time," I remark to Leecia as we head over to Memorial Hall, where it's being held.

"Yes, think of all the time we waste sleeping and eating," Leecia replies. "Seriously, though, I have to find a dance group — I'll go crazy without one."

When we get to the fair, I'm amazed at how many different groups there are. In the first fifty feet, Leecia picks up info on three different dance groups, the track team, and the Harvard band. We pass the Harvard chess club, a kite-flying club, the debate team.

"Oh," she says, suddenly veering off to another booth. I follow her. AFRICAN AMERICAN STUDENTS ALLIANCE reads the sign. Leecia picks up a flier.

"If the group is good, I'll definitely do it," she tells me as we walk away. "I was in the black students group at Andover and it absolutely *saved* me."

"Really?" I say, but Leecia is already at another booth, picking up information on intramural volleyball.

I stop to chat with Michelle, who's commanding the Premed Students Society booth.

"You should do an activity," she tells me while I search her booth for edibles. (Some of the groups are offering cookies as an enticement to learn about them.) "Med schools like to see a well-rounded candidate. A leadership position would be best."

"I'm planning to wait it out and inherit your position at the society," I joke.

Michelle makes a face. "This is serious," she says.

"Excuse me," says a girl at the booth. "How can I join this?"

I look around for Leecia but don't see her, so I start to walk on. I do want to join something, but something for me and *not* for my résumé, for once in my life.

In a corner of the gym, I see a Korean flag and, under it, a sign that says KOREAN AMERICAN STUDENTS OF HAR-VARD (KASH). Leecia seemed so excited about the African American Students Alliance; I wonder what KASH is all about.

There are a few people milling around the booth, so I walk toward them. They are all speaking in what I guess is Korean. As I get nearer, I start feeling dumber, like I'm in a foreign country. I hover for a minute, right on the perimeter of the booth. No one even looks up, so I walk on. What am I supposed to do, barge in with a "Hi"?

I stop next at the Harvard paper, the *Crimson*. I tell the roly-poly guy at the booth that I'm interested in writing.

"Writing for the *Crimson* is extremely competitive," he tells me right off. "We have a lot of really good writers on our staff. Would you like a submission form? We ask to see three manuscripts."

"You mean I have to try out just to get a chance to write for the paper?" I ask incredulously. The Arkin High paper used to beg for articles, and I don't know whether journalism is even a kind of writing I'm interested in.

"Yeah, like I said —" His attention is suddenly stolen by a pretty girl now browsing at the display. Within seconds, I'm ignored. I move on.

The Young Republicans of Harvard, the Horticulturists Club, the Baha'i Association of Harvard. I keep walking.

Another Korean flag, next to an American flag, catches my eye. Now who could *these* people be? A competing group? Under the flags sit a girl and a guy, both clad in white karate uniforms tied with black belts. HARVARD TAE KWON DO CLUB says their sign.

My curiosity piqued, I start edging forward.

The girl catches my eye and smiles. "Are you interested in tae kwon do?" she asks. She has the hair I wish I had: jet black and as thick as a curtain.

"Um, I don't know," I admit. "What is it?"

"Tae kwon do is a martial art that's like karate —"

"It's ten times better than karate," the guy next to her interrupts. "It was invented by Koreans."

"Don't listen to Ralph here," the girl says, playfully pushing him away. "Tae kwon do is *different* from karate.

· 34 ·

While karate uses a lot of hand techniques, TKD uses more kicks. I really like it because it's helped me become more flexible."

"I can put my big toe in my ear," Ralph adds helpfully.

"That's nice," I say. "What do you guys do in the club?"

"Three times a week, Master Han, the teacher, holds a class. We work on techniques and practice them in forms, which are choreographed routines. Sometimes we spar — you know, free fighting."

"Hmm," I say. I can't quite imagine fighting, hitting someone. But taking up a new sport does sound fun. And it *is* Korean.

"Come on Wednesday for the free trial class, no obligation," Ralph says. The girl makes a face and hits him again.

"The club *is* free," she says. "We meet Mondays, Wednesdays, and Fridays at seven-thirty, in the wrestling room on the third floor of the MAC — the Malkin Athletic Center. Our first session is next Wednesday."

"Maybe I'll try it out," I say, half to myself.

"Please do," the girl says. "You'll like it."

"Maybe I will," I say. I leave to find Leecia.

Chapter Six

M Y FIRST FRIDAY NIGHT, and I'm bushed — at eight o'clock.

"So what are you doing tonight?" Leecia asks as I come in from the library. She is sitting in the common room reading *Why We Can't Wait,* by Dr. Martin Luther King.

I set my bag down with a plop. In high school, I always wanted to go out, but my parents often made me study. Now my parents are half a continent away, and all I want to do is study. How did this happen?

"Actually, Leecia, I was planning to stay in. I have chem to get done before I go into lab tomorrow, and I'd like to work on my short story assignment."

"I'm staying in, too," Leecia says. "But I was wondering if you'd like to go out for coffee or ice cream — or coffee ice cream — around ten or so."

"That I can handle," I say, admittedly relieved that Leecia is studying tonight, too. Just now as I walked across campus, I passed all sorts of people in different stages of inebriation: people giggling and skipping together, people yelling under dorm windows. I couldn't help wondering if

I was missing out on something. But if I am, at least I'm not alone.

I move to our newest possession, a lumpy couch. The football players were getting rid of it, and when we asked them if we could have it, they even carried it into our room for us.

I've decided to tackle the harder assignment first: write a paragraph about home for the short stories class. I put a fresh piece of paper in front of me and write "home" at the top of it. My freshly made herb tea steams in its mug as I set it down on a coaster.

Home.

I wait.

Home. That's so easy. It's a million things.

But what is it, in one paragraph?

One paragraph that Marianne Stoeller, and perhaps the rest of the class, is going to read.

Home?

Help.

Writing should be easy, right? It's just putting one word after another down on paper.

So what makes a home a home? Our house isn't *really* our home; before we moved there, the Olesons lived in it for over thirty years.

But it's the only home I know. What makes it mine?

I think of my bedroom: yellow wallpaper, grainy ceiling, the bed at the side of the wall, facing east, where the sun comes up.

For some reason I start thinking about the patterns in the wallpaper. When I was little, I used to believe I could see bears, tigers, mermaids, sprouting out of the wall in the same way that clouds can be ships or people. I remember how I used to look at those patterns and wonder, were all the creatures inside the patterns imagining me, a little girl?

Home. Home as an imaginary wallpaper world? People will think I'm on drugs.

Home is the yellow and red wallpaper in my bedroom. The words arrange themselves in my brain.

But shouldn't I be thinking more about the house, not the weird imaginings I had as a kid?

I'm getting nowhere, I realize. The near-empty page jeers at me; I resist the temptation to crumple it up and throw it away.

I shut my eyes.

Home is the yellow and red wallpaper in my bedroom.

I make a deal with myself. I will let myself write whatever comes to mind without worrying what people will think. If it's too weird, I can throw it out.

Home is . . . The next sentence comes, then the next — pearls on a strand. When I'm done, I have a paragraph, more or less.

I read it over again, prod it, try to change words. Yes, it *is* weird. But it's even weirder that when I sit back silently, the words come rushing back: *Home is . . . Past, present, future, stillness and motion.*

From the bedroom, the Holstein clock gives off its gentle moo to signify the arrival of a new hour.

I wonder what Jessie is doing tonight. *Home is . . .*

I slip the paper into my folder and reach for my chemistry book.

Chapter Seven

THAT WEDNESDAY, I receive my first letter from Jessie.

Dear Ellen,

Boy — do I miss you! Arkin is sooo boring without you. Mike left for UMD last week, but we see each other every weekend. I like going up to Duluth 'cause there's a lot more happening. Last week we went to the Brass Rail and they had some *excellent* bands there.

I've decided to stay in Arkin and try to find a job. No luck yet — I might take some classes at the junior college if nothing comes up.

Remember how we thought Marsha Randall was dating Dr. Mikola, our favorite dentist? Well, they are *engaged!* I guess this makes up for her not getting into dental hygienists' school. I sincerely hope they move out of Arkin. By the way, did you know Dr. M. is 36? That's O-L-D.

That's it for now. Oh, Shari is *pregnant.* I sus-
pect Rocky Jukich, but she's not saying. She is
going to keep the baby. We'll see what it looks
like when it comes out (if it's wearing a jean
jacket, we'll know it's Rocky's — haha).

Love ya lots,
Jessie

P.S. Am counting the days 'til Christmas!

I sit back on my bed and watch the afternoon sun filter
into our tiny room. Outside, through the golden light and
the metallic color of falling leaves, I can see tweedy professors and backpacked students striding about. Everyone
looks so purposeful.

A tourist crouches to take a picture of the John Harvard
statue and surrounding campus. *My* campus.

I know I should appreciate this place more. There are
Nobel Prize–winners walking around here, while back
home, Jessie can't find a job. But why should I have the
privilege of being among such smart people?

Jessie still loves me. I have friends. I'm here to study,
make my mark on the world. I gather up my books. I have
two solid hours to work before dinner.

*

After dinner, all my work is finished, so I decide to attend
the tae kwon do class, just to see what it's all about. It's a
short walk to the MAC, and I find the wrestling room easily enough. Inside, a Korean flag hangs next to an American
flag on the wall, just as it did at the activities fair.

The girl I met at the fair spies me and comes over. Her hair is tied back in a thick ponytail.

"Glad you could come . . ."

"I'm Ellen," I say.

"Sook-Hee," she says. "A.k.a. Sookie."

What an interesting name. I know my Korean name is Myong-Ok, but my parents rarely call me that.

"So what do I do?" I ask, looking around. There are half a dozen people in white uniforms with different-colored belts, and another half-dozen of us in street clothes.

"Do you have a uniform?" she asks.

"No," I say. "Should I?"

"Of course not, but sometimes people get hand-me-downs from siblings."

I smile at this thought. Michelle, with her utter scorn of all things noncerebral, is the last person I can see doing tae kwon do, or any sport.

"The uniform costs thirty dollars," Sookie says. "But you don't have to commit today. You can just watch the class if you want."

"No, I'll do it," I say, strangely sure of myself. "But I don't have the money right now."

"No problem," Sookie says. She picks out a plastic-wrapped uniform from a pile and we go into the locker room together.

My new outfit is white and as starchy as rice. Sookie shows me how to tie the white belt, and she writes my name in funny characters on the neck.

"Is this Korean?" I say, without stopping to think how stupid I sound. What else would it be?

"Yep," Sookie says with a nod.

We go back into the wrestling room and I see some other novices, barefoot and white-belted like me.

Ralph, the guy I also met earlier, brings the class to order. "Master Han sends his apologies that he couldn't make it today," he says. "He instructed me to go over some of the basics."

We start off by doing some warming-up exercises. I'm delighted to see that my high school gymnastics experience has paid off by leaving me nice and flexible.

Next Ralph shows us how to stand. "The basic tae kwon do stance is the front stance," he says as he demonstrates. "Forward leg bent, back leg locked, one shoulder width apart."

The higher belts do this easily. We white belts lurch into various versions of what Ralph has shown us.

"Ellen," Sookie says to me, "keep your front leg bent a little more — great."

We practice this stance over and over. The black belts patiently go around correcting us each time.

Next we learn how to punch.

"All you do," Ralph says, "is push your punch out, and at the last second tense your fist and flip it over. Oh yeah, pull in your opposite arm at the same speed, and remember to keep the upper body stationary."

We all try to copy Ralph again.

"And don't lean!" he exhorts, and I see that all of us white belts are doing exactly that.

Whew! How *did* the Koreans come up with this?

We spend the rest of the class just trying to get the hang

of the simple, straightforward punch. We end with situps and pushups.

When we're dismissed, Ralph and another guy playfully spar, throwing punches, blocks, and spinning kicks at each other.

"How'd you like it?" Sookie asks, sitting next to me.

"It was great," I say, although my right hamstring is tightening up. "I just feel like a klutz."

"It takes time to get used to the movement," she says.

We watch the guys. Ralph screams like a banshee and leaps up in a kick. The other guy ducks and they resume their fight on the ground. Amazing.

"So how are you liking Harvard?" Sookie asks me.

"It's okay, I guess," I say. I can't say I really *like* living with a bathroom that never seems quite clean, or eating institutional food. Or that I enjoy the I'm-the-smartest/richest/greatest/best attitude so many people seem to have. But isn't that the point? You're not supposed to like Harvard, you're just supposed to get through it, right?

"What dorm are you in?" Sookie asks.

"Weld," I tell her.

"Oh, Jae-Chun is in Weld," she says. "He's another freshman joining the club. Do you know him, Jae-Chun Kim?"

"No," I say. "Weld is a big dorm."

Sookie nods. "Harvard is a big place in general. You have to be careful not to get lost."

*

"How was it?" Leecia asks. We've returned to the dorm at the same time, me from tae kwon do, Leecia from tryouts for her dance group.

"Pretty fun," I say. "How was your audition?"

"I think I danced okay," she says. "I really want to get into this group. They do a lot of really original stuff in modern dance and jazz — and it's all women of color."

"I'm sure you'll get it," I say. I haven't actually ever seen Leecia dance, but I'm certain she's good. She has a muscular, graceful body that looks like it was *made* to dance.

"If I do get it, I think the African American Students Alliance will be the only other activity I'll do," Leecia declares. "The track team looks like a lot of work, and the band looks kind of fun but not too musical; I think most people just want to party."

"What do they do in the African American Students Alliance?"

"They get away from the white elitism that permeates this place," she says, a bemused smile creeping onto her face. "Ya know, sometimes you just need to have a place to hang out comfortably with your own type." Leecia sits on the floor, splits her legs into a V, and starts stretching.

"Leecia, do you have any good dancer's stretches you can show me?" I ask. "I want to get more flexible for tae kwon do — especially my poor stressed hamstrings."

"I know a ton of those, sweetie," Leecia says. "In fact they're two-person stretches. We can help each other out."

Leecia tells me to sit back to back with her, and we take turns pushing each other's upper body down.

"So what was it like growing up in Minnesota?" she asks. Her voice is slightly muffled by her knees.

"It was nice," I say. "The area I'm from, northern Minnesota, is especially pretty, with all the lakes."

"Did you ever experience any racism living up there?"

My hamstring twinges.

"Uh, yeah," I say.

"I'm just curious," Leecia says. "As an African American, I always expect it. I was just wondering what it's like for an Asian."

I shrug. "I think most of the people in Arkin were good people. There were just a few bad ones, and we were in kind of a weird situation, being the only minority family in town."

"Wow — your town was all white?" Leecia asks. "Did you ever have crosses burned on your lawn or anything?"

"Oh, nothing like that," I say. "Mostly small stuff, like being called names in the hall."

Leecia stops mid-stretch and turns to face me. "That's not small stuff," she says. "It's more like death by a thousand cuts — same result."

"What's the worst thing that ever happened to you?"

Leecia pauses. "Having been black all my life, it's hard to decide," she finally says. "But I think it would be the day when I was walking around town in Andover. It was a beautiful day, and I was just thinking about how happy I was to be alive. Then I hear this screeching noise, and this car almost runs me over. When I look up, the car has stopped. I'm getting set to run. Then I see spit flying out an open window and someone — the car was filled with local yahoos — holds up this cardboard sign that says 'nigger.' Then they drove off."

"Oh, Leecia," I say. We have stopped stretching for a moment; now we are sitting back to back, our elbows still linked.

Leecia chuckles softly. "For the first few minutes, I was

just really relieved that they weren't rapists. Then I realized what had happened to me, that these guys really *were* rapists, even though they didn't touch me physically. I just felt so sad and angry and useless, like I wanted to kill them and cry at the same time. They were way gone by then, so I went home and cried."

"Oh, Leecia," I say again. Her back is a warm, firm tree trunk next to mine. She is incredibly strong. Someday, I want to tell her about my scar, how I got it from a racist girl. But not now. Now would seem too much like one-upmanship, so I'll wait.

Chapter Eight

"I GOT IT!" Leecia yells as she comes into the suite, grabs my arms, and swings me around. "I'm going to be in that dance group, One in the Heart!"

"That's so fabulous!" I hug her. "You're going to be great."

"You'll be getting stretchy right along with me, dear," Leecia says, doing a pirouette. "Post-studying stretches every night from now on."

"Definitely."

That afternoon when I'm at the Coop, I buy Leecia a mug that has a hippo in ballet shoes to celebrate her triumph. I also buy Jessie a little Harvard magnet, a tacky plastic one that I know she will love.

I leave the Coop with a full heart, thinking how wonderful friends are.

*

On Monday I return to the wrestling room.

Master Han is there. He is a tiny man with silver hair. His black belt is so old it's fraying at the ends. He has a serene look to his eyes, which I hope means that he'll be patient with us white belts.

A boy with a red belt comes in, greeting everyone. I've seen people with yellow belts, blue belts, and green belts. He's the first red belt I've seen. He waves to Sookie and me, and as I wave back, I recognize him as the black-haired guy from our dorm. Perhaps he's the Jae-Chun that Sookie was telling me about.

Before I can ask her, Master Han claps his hands, and everyone scrambles to line up, the black belts in front, the other colored belts following, and the white belts filling in the rear. The red-belt boy, I notice, takes the place right behind the black belts.

This same guy then starts the class. He says something in Korean, and everyone bows to the master. He says something else, and everyone bows toward the flags.

"White belts," Master Han says, "watch the higher belts do the *kemaseh* stance. This is what we do to begin the class."

At Master Han's command, the tae kwon do veterans step into what I can only describe as a graceful, bowlegged cowboy stance. From there, they punch in unison, and at the end they yell *Hi-yah!* or something like that, all together. The noise in the small wrestling room is deafening.

"*Kemaseh* is the horseback-riding stance," Master Han says, demonstrating slowly for us. "From here, you do the straightforward punches you learned last week. At the end, I say *kihap*, which means 'spirit yell.' "

We white belts try the *kemaseh* a few times, then we do it together as a class. Punch, punch, punch. When Master

Han tells us to *kihap,* I yell as loudly as I can; it feels wonderful.

At the end of class, the red-belt boy closes with more Korean, and we all bow to the master.

I sit on the side and stretch for my cool-down. Sookie is practicing what is called a form. She is doing punches, blocks, and high kicks in the air, moving deliberately across the floor. I'm not sure what it's supposed to look like, but she appears sure and strong.

"Hi, Ellen." The red-belt boy is beside me.

"Uh, hi," I say, surprised. "How'd you know my name?"

"It's on your uniform, right here," he says, tapping the place on my neck where Sookie wrote my name in Korean characters.

I start, for some reason, then recover.

"I can't read Korean," I say.

"No kidding?" the boy says. "You're Korean, right?"

"Yes, but where I grew up there weren't any other Koreans; my parents figured I'd never use it."

"Sounds logical," he says, his eyes looking thoughtful. "Everyone I ever knew went to Korean school on weekends, whether they wanted to or not."

"Where are you from?" I ask.

"L.A.," he says. "Land of *mucho* Koreans. So, did you ever want to learn?"

"I haven't really given it much thought," I say. This isn't quite true: when I was five or six and just beginning to learn to read in English, I found some Korean children's books in the house, and I remember wanting very badly to know what they said. I felt sad when Mom said, "No, Ellen,

English is your language, not Korean." But that was a long time ago.

"Korean is pretty straightforward," the boy says. "The written stuff especially. You could learn the alphabet in an hour, easy."

"Really?" I say. "I thought you had to learn thousands of characters."

"That's Chinese," he says. "There are some Chinese ideographs in the Korean language, but the alphabet is actually phonetic, like the good old ABC."

"What's your name?" I ask suddenly.

"Jae-Chun," he says, pointing to the characters on his uniform's neck. "You can call me J.C., or Jae." He grins. One of his front teeth is slightly crooked, giving him a friendly, snaggle-toothed look.

Just then Master Han walks up to us. Jae bows respectfully to him, so I do the same. Master Han starts talking to Jae in Korean. Jae looks at me apologetically, but I bow out and retire to the locker room.

When I come back out, changed, Jae is gone.

Chapter Nine

I CAN'T BELIEVE how much time I have to spend in lab for chem class. In high school, once a week we'd have a "lab day," and even then we'd spend only part of class in lab. Now I go to lab for hours outside of lecture — even longer if my experiments don't work. I've worn safety goggles to the point where I have an angry red mask around my face — the true sign of a premed nerd.

I find myself looking forward to tae kwon do. It's such good exercise, the stretching feels wonderful, and now I know two nice people, Sookie and Jae — two people who also happen to be Korean, like me.

In the next class we learn how to kick, and we practice it on porkchop-shaped leather pads that the black belts hold for everybody.

"Go for it," Sookie urges when it's my turn. "As hard as you can."

I kick it, and the leather target responds with a reassuring splat. Exhilarated, I run to the back of the line.

After class, Jae comes over to me again. "Up for learning

some Korean?" he asks. He is wearing a white T-shirt under his uniform, and it's sticking slightly to his broad and defined chest. He reminds me, somewhat incongruously, of Tomper.

"Sure," I say. I can't think of any reason not to.

I go into the locker room, take a quick shower, and change. Jae is waiting when I come out. He has a New York Yankees baseball cap plastered over his wet hair. He hoists his gym bag onto his shoulder.

"*Anyonghaseo*," he says.

"Huh?" I say.

"*Anyonghaseo*," he says again. "It means hello."

"Oh," I say. "Then an-yong . . ."

"*Anyonghaseo*."

"*Anyonghaseo*."

"Very good."

We make the short walk back to Weld, then head to the common room on the first floor. To get there, we pass by Irwin's apartment.

"Have you ever been in to see him?" Jae asks quietly, motioning toward Irwin's closed door.

"Once," I say, when we're out of range.

"I was really bummed about something right when school started," Jae says, his face looking suddenly serious. "I went to him and all he said, over and over, was 'It's okay to be depressed here; this is Harvard — everyone feels this way.' Well, I know most people here weren't feeling the way *I* felt."

I want to ask him what was wrong, but I can't find a way to do it without sounding nosy. I barely know him, after all.

"He's not a bad guy, though," Jae goes on. "I'm sure it's tough being in grad school, being married, and having to look after us. I just think he's sort of ineffective as a counselor."

I nod.

"Anyway," Jae says, pulling out a piece of paper, "we're here to learn Korean, not mope."

The paper has all sorts of lines, angles, boxes, and circles on it. "Cursive Korean looks fancier than this," Jae says. "But this format is the easiest to learn."

He goes over the different sounds each character makes, and he's right, it *is* extremely logical. The sounds depend on the line — which way it's going, how many lines there are.

"This is easier than *our* alphabet," I say.

Jae's black eyes shine. "See, I told you," he says. He starts writing some simple words for me to sound out. *Ellen, kihap, Jae.* I can read!

"Here, try these," he says.

"*Cha, uyu, kim* . . . Hey — I've heard *uyu* before!" I exclaim.

"Can you remember?" Jae says excitedly. "It's a really common word with kids."

Uyu, I think. *Uyu.*

"Oh — milk!" I practically yell.

"You're right," Jae says, patting my shoulder. I feel the warmth of his fingers, briefly.

As I remember the word *uyu,* however, I also remember Father, uncharacteristically loud, scolding Mom, and Mom firing back that my learning one Korean word wouldn't accent my English forever. How old was I then, three? This makes me think of home, home as something that's irretrievably gone. I'll never be that young again, never be able to learn Korean from my parents.

"You okay?" Jae says, gently peering into my eyes.

"Oh, yeah," I say. "I was weirded out by a memory."

"Want to talk about it?"

I shake my head.

"Well," he says, getting up. "You've been a quick study." He hands me the sheet with the Korean characters on it. "For you to keep."

"Thanks," I say. "Are you going to teach me how to say goodbye?"

Jae's eyes fasten on me for a second.

"No," he says finally. I'm not sure how I'm supposed to react to this.

"Okay," I say. "*Hasta luego,* then."

*

"My," says Leecia when I walk into the suite, "that tae kwon do must be good for you. Your cheeks are all pink."

"Really?" I say. Tae kwon do ended at least an hour ago.

That night I put the Korean alphabet sheet that Jae gave me under my pillow. Perhaps I can learn by osmosis. Perhaps.

Chapter Ten

"ELLEN, WHY DON'T YOU come eat dinner at my house tonight?" Michelle's recorded voice warbles slightly in Leecia's answering machine. "I'm sorry that I've been so busy and haven't had time to see you."

I call Michelle back and go over to her upperclassmen dorm, Lowell House. I like the fact that the houses have their own dining rooms.

"So how are your classes?" Michelle asks, the minute we sit down with our food.

"They're okay," I say, although I have hardly been graded in anything yet. "Mom and Father don't expect me to get all A's here, do they?"

"Mom and Father don't expect you to do anything," Michelle says. "But keep in mind that there *are* people who apply to med school who have all A's, including people from Harvard."

Including people like her. Michelle has an almost perfect GPA.

"I'm a little sick of chem lab," I admit.

"The labs are important," Michelle says. "Fight for every point, and don't be fooled by the teaching assistants who seem buddy-buddy. You'll need every point."

"Leecia, my roommate, said the same thing," I remark. At Harvard, you go to huge lecture halls to receive the pearls of wisdom from gray-haired professors, but you are often actually taught in smaller classes called "sections" by teaching assistants who are graduate students. I would have assumed that since the TAs are students, too, they'd have some empathy, but I guess they are notoriously hard graders.

"So how's the roommate situation?" Michelle asks.

"Leecia's great," I say, brightening. "She's invited me home for Thanksgiving."

"That's good," Michelle says. "I hated my freshman roommates."

"But you're best friends with Jenny."

"With Jenny, yes, but remember, there were five of us. The other three were a group of ditzes. I'm glad you and Leecia seem to be well matched."

I think of my routine with Leecia: most meals together, chats over tea before bed, weekends in each other's company. Study, study, study.

"I'm glad, too," I say.

Michelle smiles. "Remember when you were so reluctant to come here? I'd say you're fitting in pretty well."

I smile back. Coming from her, that's a pretty big compliment.

Chapter Eleven

AFTER THE NEXT FEW tae kwon do classes, Jae waits for me each time and asks if I want to learn more Korean. I say yes, and we go back to the study room.

I don't know very much about Jae except that he's from L.A. and he speaks Korean. I've figured out that I think he's handsome. After watching him at tae kwon do and now sitting around with him, I feel . . . I don't know. I guess I feel the way I haven't felt since I left Tomper. I didn't realize it would happen again so soon.

Tomper recently wrote me a letter that was very neutral, but I have the feeling he was waiting for me to be a little more intimate, and then maybe torrents of old feelings would gush out from him. His letter was mostly chatty, about guys snoring in bunks, practical jokes. But he signed the letter "love," which he never did in high school; back then, he'd just sign his notes with a plain old "Tomper," or at most with a "see ya" attached.

I wrote back, a little guiltily, signing with "your friend,

Ellen," ~~which *I* also never did before. In high school, I al-~~ ways signed my notes "love."

*

My premed classes continue to be hard, but I'm not as intimidated as I was the first couple of days. It seems that some of the people I thought were so smart really just like to talk a lot. And if they're all as confident as they appear, then why, a few days before our first quiz in chem, were the answers to a problem set stolen from the bulletin board in the lab? (They were replaced promptly, this time in a locked glass case.)

The only course in which I don't know where I stand is short stories. The week after I submitted my "home" paragraph, Marianne Stoeller selected a few of the assignments to read and discuss in class.

The lead piece was written by the ripped jeans girl. Only this girl doesn't wear ripped jeans anymore; now she wears clothes that are loose and flowing. Once I even saw her wind a lilac-colored scarf around her neck.

Marianne Stoeller had us discuss that "home" piece and others. We talked about what they meant, pointed out possible metaphors they contained, and made comments about the style. Marianne Stoeller didn't directly criticize or praise the works but instead just kept the discussion going. However, it was clear that she liked the first "home" piece a lot, and the author knew it, too. And why not, if the girl has already been published?

I worked like a dog on assignments two and three, but my work hasn't been picked yet — and I'm dying of suspense.

*

"The Head of the Charles is coming up," Leecia says, looking up from her organizer. "Want to go?"

"Sounds like fun," I say. "I've never seen a crew race before."

"People come from all over the country," Leecia says. "We'll have a blast."

So the day before the race, Leecia and I make a rare trip off-campus to shop for a picnic lunch.

"It's weird being in the real world again," Leecia remarks, looking around. "I keep forgetting that people *live* in Cambridge."

"Leecia, there is life beyond Harvard," I say.

We pass by a public high school, which must have just gotten out because the area is swarming with students laughing, shouting, pushing. A particularly rowdy bunch gets shoved into us, and instead of saying "Excuse me," they say, "Fuck you, bitches — watch out!" and walk on.

"Wow, I must be getting old," I say to Leecia. "I don't remember anyone being so loud and rude at my high school."

"I don't either," Leecia says. "And how about their language?"

Leecia continues to watch the kids as they are absorbed by the surrounding neighborhood. Some disappear into stores that have hand-lettered signs saying "Three students at a time only."

"You know, as much as I hated leaving my friends in Balto," Leecia says, "I'm glad my parents sent me away to school. Who knows what would have become of me if I'd stayed and gone to a public school."

"I went to a public school," I remind her.

"That's true," Leecia says. "But your high school was in a rural area, right?"

"Well, we had our problems with drugs and stuff like that, but I guess not to the extent of most city schools, with crack and twelve-year-olds bringing guns to school."

"Or killing MIT students," Leecia says, referring to a newspaper article we'd read about some local high school students who mugged and murdered an MIT student because, in their words, they "were bored."

Leecia and I come upon a grocery-deli and go in. A bell over the door tinkles to announce our arrival. There are some students inside buying soda and candy. Leecia and I stroll over to the cheese counter.

"They have a pretty good selection here," I say, looking at the industrial-size logs of cheese. "Should we get crackers, too?"

"Sure, I'll find some," Leecia says.

I study the assortment and decide that Vermont cheddar and Monterey Jack sound good. Maybe some cold cuts, too. I press the bell on the counter, and it rings jarringly through the store. I wait a few minutes, then press it again.

Leecia reappears, carrying a box of Stoned Wheat Thins. She is followed closely by a short Asian lady in a stained white butcher's apron.

Leecia stops, turns around, and glares at the lady. The lady glares back.

"You gonna buy that?" the woman says.

Leecia doesn't answer her but instead walks over to me and slowly, deliberately, hands me the crackers. The lady appears behind the cheese case.

"Can I help you?" she says to me.

I put in our order, all the while casting inquiring glances at Leecia. Something very weird is going on.

"Are you okay?" I ask as we leave the store.

"No," Leecia says, shaking her head.

"What's the matter?"

"Didn't you see that woman following me?" Leecia says, small fires lit in her eyes. "Koreans — no offense to you — always do this to me! They're convinced all black people steal."

"She was Korean?" I say. Now, how would Leecia know, if I couldn't tell?

"Believe me, I've been in enough Korean groceries in New York and D.C. to know," Leecia says. "You saw her practically stepping on my heels, right? She was just waiting for me to put that box of crackers up my shirt. She didn't even pretend, say 'Can I help you?' or something like that. It makes me so mad."

I replay the tape of my memory. I see the woman following Leecia up the aisle, asking her if she's going to buy the stuff. What else did she think Leecia was going to do? And if the lady was so worried about people stealing, it would have made more sense to keep on eye on me, since I was carrying the huge backpack.

"That's terrible, Leecia," I say. "She shouldn't have treated you like that."

Leecia sighs. "How come no one assumes that I'm a dean's list Harvard student? The other day in the Gap, I swear they had a whole platoon of undercover officers casing me."

If someone immediately became suspicious of me just because I'm Asian, I'd be furious. It's true that a lot of the students from the neighborhood high school are black, and maybe the storeowners have had problems with shoplifting — hence the signs. But that doesn't mean that the proprietor should look at each black person with suspicion. No one suspects all whites when a *white* person commits a crime, for heaven's sake.

"Come on, Leecia," I say, taking her arm and stepping out from the shadow into the sun. "Don't let that stupid lady bother you."

We stroll on the now uncrowded sidewalks, and I'm relieved to see Leecia's face soften into its normal cheerful expression.

We pass a thrift shop, and I notice a beautiful old-fashioned quilt in the window.

"Hey, Leecia," I say. Then I see that she's eyeing the quilt, too.

"To sit on," she says.

"For our four years here," I add.

We look delightedly at each other and rush into the store.

"How much is that quilt in the window?" Leecia sings to the elderly woman behind the counter. The woman looks at us both as if we might be a little crazy, but she stoops into the window to check.

"Ten dollars, girls," she says.

Leecia already has her wallet out. I put a hand on her arm. "I'll pay half," I say. "It'll be a joint purchase."

"A friendship quilt," Leecia agrees, putting five dollars on the counter.

Brimming with excitement, Leecia and I step out into the still-warm autumn afternoon. All of a sudden, I am filled with good feeling — happy just to be alive.

Of course, whenever I feel this spontaneously joyful, I'm reminded that at a later time I will inevitably feel worse.

But now, even that thought doesn't trouble me.

Chapter Twelve

THE HEAD OF THE CHARLES day starts out dark and ominous-looking, the sky heavy with what could be cold, chilly rain.

"It'll clear up," Leecia says optimistically as she peers out the window.

We both put on our Harvard T-shirts and pack up the picnic stuff. I invited Michelle to come with us, but she was planning to use the down time in the lab to catch up on her work — a very Michelle thing to do.

Leecia and I step outside. It's freezing, but not yet raining. We try to be brave, for about two seconds, then we run back in for our Harvard sweatshirts.

"It'll clear up," Leecia says again as we head out for the second time.

The weather doesn't seem to have dampened the attendance. There are people walking all around, vendors selling T-shirts, buses marked "Special" pulling in.

Irwin arranged a spot where people from our dorm can sit together, but Leecia and I decide to find our own.

Walking up the banks a bit, we come to a place that's comfortable and has a good view, so we set our stuff down.

"I think I see the sun peeking out there," I say, pointing. Sure enough, the sun is breaking out of the clouds, light penetrating the gloom.

"What did I tell you?" Leecia says.

"Leecia," says a voice. Leecia turns.

"Wendy!" she yells. She jumps up to embrace a fragile-looking girl with close-cropped hair.

"I should have called," the girl says. "But I somehow figured I'd find you."

"Oh my God," says Leecia. "Ellen, this is my friend Wendy from high school."

"Hi," says Wendy. She has a Howard University sweatshirt on. "Leecia, you know who else is here? Brice and Kevin."

"Brice and Kevin? No way!" squeals Leecia. "Brice went to Michigan, I thought."

"He did. He's a stowaway with the crew team."

"A mini-reunion," Leecia says in wonderment. "This is fantastic."

"They're right over there," Wendy says, pointing. "Want to go say hi?"

"Umm . . ." Leecia looks at me, at all our stuff.

"Go ahead, Leecia, I'll watch the stuff," I say.

"No, I'll catch up to you guys later," Leecia says. "Why don't we meet at three at Out-of-Town News?"

"Will do," Wendy says, waving.

"Those guys — and Teisha, my friend at Wellesley — are all friends from the black students group at Andover,"

Leecia says to me. "Boy, did we stick together like glue."

"Did you have any Asians there?" I ask.

"Oh, sure," Leecia says. "There are tons of Asian Americans at all the good schools."

How did Michelle and I grow up in isolation when there seem to be so many Asians around? What would my life be like if I had grown up speaking Korean, going to tae kwon do classes? Jae and Sookie have been doing all of that since they were little kids, and they seem so comfortable with being Korean, as if it's part of their skin, not a big pulsating question mark the way it is for me.

Maybe someday I'll figure all of this out, I think, as Leecia and I watch the boats go by. It's so beautiful, the way they seem to glide over the water.

A team in Crimson jerseys with dollar signs on their backs row by; people standing on the banks cheer them on. "Harvard Business School," Leecia says with a snort.

The sun warms up enough for us to shed our sweatshirts. We eat our lunch and sip the wine that an upperclassman was sneaky enough to buy for us. I think of Michelle working diligently in the dark and lonely lab, and I hope she's having fun.

I see Jae, and I call out to him. He smiles when he sees me, and comes over.

"Leecia, this is Jae," I say. "He's the one teaching me Korean and helping me with tae kwon do."

"I'm hardly teaching Ellen either one," Jae says. Today he is wearing a light jacket and a Dodgers baseball cap. "I just show her, and she picks it right up."

"Nice to meet you, Jae," Leecia says. "Want some wine?"

"Thanks. Very elegant," Jae says, taking the proffered glass. We are using "borrowed" Union ones.

Jae, Leecia, and I sit back and watch the afternoon go by. Jae takes off his jacket.

A little before three, Leecia jumps up.

"Got to go meet Wendy and the gang," she says. "Want to come, Ellen? My friends would love to meet you."

I can barely move, I'm so drugged with sun and wine.

"Uh, mind if I pass?" I mumble. "I'm stuck here."

"Of course not," Leecia says. "Just don't forget the quilt and our lovely Union glasses."

"I won't," I say.

"Ellen, mind if I stay?" Jae asks after Leecia leaves.

"Of course not," I say, just now noticing that we are lying rather close together.

The water of the Charles River looks very blue. The wine is warm on my tongue.

"Jae, why do you always wear a baseball cap?" I say, emboldened by wine. "You have such nice hair."

I hear him shift beside me.

"Makes me look less like an Asian geek, I guess," he says.

"You're not a geek," I say. "Look how good you are at tae kwon do."

Jae whistles softly through his teeth. "Yeah, but even there, did you ever notice how all the macho martial arts stars are white? Jean-Claude Van Damme, Steven Segal, that blond android Dolf Lungren."

"But what about Bruce Lee?"

"Sure," Jae says. "He *invented* the whole genre. But even

then, when he appeared on screen he was emasculated. His non-Asian costars always got the women, and Bruce was always up in his room meditating or something."

I want to tell Jae that no person with adequate vision would ever consider him a geek, but instead I just flop onto my back and look at the sky, which has finally, definitively won over the clouds.

At one point, Jae and I roll over at the same time. Our hands touch and then stay together — a mutual Velcro effect. I don't feel like I've taken his hand or like he's taken mine, but here we are, holding hands.

Jae's hand is strong; it has a soft, broken-in-leather feel, like an old baseball glove.

"Can you break boards with these?" I ask, running a finger over a callus on his first knuckle.

"Yes," he says, turning to face me.

The next thing I know, we're kissing. There is sun, or something, in my eyes.

"Ellen!"

First I see Michelle's Reeboked feet, then the rest of her. Her hair is slightly disheveled, and she's carrying an armload of lab notebooks.

Michelle? Why now?

"Uh, hi, Michelle," I say, making a conscious effort not to wipe my mouth. "How was lab?"

"I've just finished," she says. "So I thought I'd walk back along the Charles to see if I could find you."

"Well, you did," I say.

"Where's Leecia?"

"She went to meet some friends."

Michelle looks at Jae with a "who's this?" look, but when I introduce them, she looks at something over her shoulder.

"Nice to meet you, Michelle," Jae says. Then he turns to me, touching my elbow. "Ellen, I've got to go. I'll see you in tae kwon do."

"Okay." I nod, wanting so much for him to stay but knowing I could never ask him to.

"Your new boyfriend?" Michelle queries, a bit snidely, as she automatically starts helping me pick up the picnic stuff.

"Michelle, I don't want to talk about it."

"I'd watch out for guys here," Michelle says. "They're after one thing. You might think it's fun now, but just wait until you see him sleeping with all your friends."

"Are you talking from experience?"

"Ellen, don't get sarcastic. I'm trying to give you some advice. And what's this about tae kwon do?"

"I'm in the Tae Kwon Do Club," I say simply.

"*That's* the activity you picked?" Michelle says incredulously. "Ellen, I've heard people get hurt all the time in those martial arts clubs. Have you stopped to consider what might happen if you hurt your hand and, say, couldn't become a surgeon?"

"Michelle, at my level, the only way I could hurt myself is if I slipped in the locker room," I say with a sigh. "Besides, it's fun, and it *is* Korean. Mom and Father should be glad I'm exploring my roots here in college."

"That guy you were with," Michelle says. "Was he Korean?"

"Yeah — you can't fault me for that," I say. Michelle's

· 69 ·

first boyfriend here was Korean, too. Perhaps we're both reacting to eighteen years of whitebread Arkin.

"I didn't say anything," she says, a slightly mischievous look in her eyes. That's Michelle — you never know what to expect.

"How about stopping by our dorm for a hot cup of tea before heading back to Lowell?" I suggest.

"I think I could spare a minute," Michelle says.

Laden with the remains of a good picnic and a good day, Michelle and I head back toward campus.

Chapter Thirteen

O N FRIDAY, I have math and chemistry and a long bio section, so by that night I'm really looking forward to tae kwon do — and seeing Jae.

"There aren't many people here," I remark to Sookie, as I survey the sparse crowd. Jae isn't here either, and now that I think of it, he wasn't here last Friday.

"Just us diehards," she says as Master Han brings the class to attention.

Jae doesn't show up at all; after class, I casually ask Sookie, "Jae doesn't come on Fridays, does he?"

"Nope," Sookie says, shaking her head. "We have KASH — Korean American Students of Harvard — events on Fridays sometimes, and he doesn't come to those either. I think he may have a girlfriend at Barnard whom he visits on the weekends."

A girlfriend! My heart sinks inside my chest. I hope Sookie doesn't notice.

Boy, did I misjudge him. Under the influence of a little wine and sun, he turns into a cheater. I guess it's good that

Michelle interrupted us before we went any further. I guess she was right about Harvard guys.

*

"I'd give him the benefit of the doubt," Leecia says to me. We're at a party in another dorm, but already we are cordoned off by ourselves, discussing probably exactly what we would be discussing if we were back in our room.

"But Sookie says she thinks he has a girlfriend."

"She *thinks*," Leecia says.

"Well, she's in this Korean students group with him," I tell her, "so she must know him fairly well."

"It's still only speculation," Leecia says. "If you ask me, Jae doesn't seem like the playboy type. Why don't you just ask him?"

"Ask him?" I say, sitting down on the couch. A guy sitting at the far end of it smiles at me. "I can't ask him that."

Leecia raises her eyebrow. "If you don't ask, you won't know," she says.

*

On Monday I see Jae in tae kwon do. He smiles and waves at me, and after class he asks me if I want to study some more Korean.

I say yes because I do.

Jae has made up a vocabulary sheet to help me start learning real words: apple, house, tea. We are both sitting on the couch, as we did last time. Jae leans close to me in his friendly way, but I carefully keep myself a good distance away, like a bird spacing itself from another bird on a telephone wire. I try not to look at him, because there are so many things about him I was starting to like: his broad shoulders, his crooked front tooth, his eyes blacker than onyx.

By the end of "class," I can say *This is an apple, this is a chair.* I am very proud of myself.

I look at Jae, perhaps hoping he'll blurt out something about his girlfriend, but he's only smiling at me encouragingly.

"Thanks Jae, I appreciate it," I say, my voice attired in formality. I gather my stuff and return to the suite.

*

Midterm crush seems to fall on us with the same abruptness that Dorothy's house fell on the Wicked Witch of the East.

In our dorm, computer keyboards clack late into the night. Kids have started wearing old sweats and flannel shirts — as close as you can get to wearing pajamas in public — all the time, even to class. Leecia is writing a lot of papers, and I have tons of formulas and phyla to memorize.

In my short stories class, we don't have anything midterm-related, but there I have a unique problem: none of my works has been selected for class yet, even though I keep trying harder and harder with each one.

In last week's class, Marianne Stoeller said we were going to start writing real stories, not just doing exercises. This week we're supposed to turn in a story on anything we want, ten pages or less.

I keep feeling that Marianne Stoeller likes everyone's work except mine. People in my class seem to lead such interesting lives, judging from their submissions. The lilac-scarf girl gives her pieces great titles like "The Rape of Persephone." Other people write about characters having affairs in exotic lands or hanging out in New York jazz clubs. I wish I knew how well I'm doing.

I still go to tae kwon do as often as possible, for the tension-relieving effects of it, but I use the midterm crush as an excuse not to see Jae after class. I want to learn Korean, but there are other ways. Maybe I'll take real lessons next semester.

*

"I can't do this!" I wail, crumpling up the blank piece of paper in frustration. "I have absolutely *no* capacity for creativity."

Leecia looks up from her book, *The Autobiography of Malcolm X.*

"Come on, Ellen," she says. "You're such a wit — there must be a virtual caldron of creativity bubbling under all that."

"I can't write," I moan.

"You've written before," Leecia says.

"Stuff that the teacher doesn't want to subject the class to," I say.

"You don't know that for sure," Leecia says.

"Why else am I about the only one who hasn't had her work critiqued?"

"*Are* you the only one?"

"There's one other person."

"So there," Leecia says. "I think you're reading too much into it. Why don't you just let it all hang out, have fun? This class is your elective, after all."

"Let it all hang out," I repeat, looking at Leecia. Is she serious?

"Why not?" she says, going back to her book.

· 74 ·

I stare at a fresh page. I have actually had an idea for a story about a father and a daughter. Basically, the girl gets yelled at by her father, and she wonders what her father was like as a little boy, if he did the same kinds of things. I've been putting off this idea, though, first because it seems childish and dumb, and second because the incident really happened to me. I feel like it's a cop-out merely to transcribe your life and call it fiction.

But what if I gave the girl a new name, changed some details?

I name the girl Joy. "If only Joy knew what was going to happen to her that day." The first sentence. It sounds okay to me.

In my mind's eye I can see a small drama unfolding, like a movie, but narrower — more like watching TV on Leecia's Sony Watchman. I see the girl — myself, almost — doing things. I write about what she's doing, what she's thinking. Some of the writing seems silly, but I try to let myself go. I'll correct it later.

When I'm done, I have a six-page story. Not bad.

*

"Now that we're getting into the meat of writing stories," Marianne Stoeller says to us in class, "I'll be meeting with each of you individually to discuss your work."

I hand in my story, "Like Father, Like Daughter," with a sinking heart. When I looked at it again, it seemed weird — did I write that? But it is too late to do another, so I just let it go.

Marianne Stoeller reads the names of the people whose submissions we're going to critique. Mine is there. Now I wish it weren't.

I sweat and sweat through the other people's pieces. This assignment was to write a story or character sketch of only one page. For mine, I made up a macabre story that was inspired by Flannery O'Connor's "A Good Man is Hard to Find" and Shirley Jackson's "The Lottery." "Coming Up Roses" is about a woman who wants things to "come up roses," and this happens — but only after she dies and a rosebush is planted on her grave.

"I like the title," says a guy who always smells of an odd brand of cigarettes. "It's quite clever." I mentally shower him with thanks.

No one else says anything. I try not to look at anyone's face.

"So what do people think of the narrative, the pacing?" Marianne Stoeller gently prods.

The lilac scarf girl comes charging in: "Totally derivative of Flannery O'Connor," she says. "But without the clincher ending. This one has an ending that's so predictable, it reeks of cliché."

There is a murmur going around the class that seems to be one of assent. If I could slink out of class and never return, I would. This woman has stomped on my soul.

Marianne Stoeller moves on to the next piece. At the end of class I find out that I am going to be one of the first people meeting with her next week in private session.

What could my grade be? I can almost hear Michelle saying *I told you so, I told you so.* I've been working so hard, only to be shot down. Am I the only person here who's deluded herself so, confusing effort with talent?

I'm not looking forward to the meeting, that's for sure.

Chapter Fourteen

"Now that midterms are almost over," Jae says to me after tae kwon do class, "do you feel like continuing the Korean studies?"

He is crouched down near me, leaning in flirtatiously. What is he trying to do? I don't know what game he's playing, but I'm not going along with it.

"No." The word comes out of my mouth like a shot.

"Why not?" he asks.

"I'm too busy," I reply, getting up rudely.

But the minute I get into the shower and cool my hot head, I realize how rude and childish I've been. No one, not even an attempted two-timer, deserves that.

When I leave the gym, I see Jae walking a few lengths ahead of me. His pace is brisk, but I struggle to catch up.

"Jae!" I say as I pull up beside him. He stops, surprised, and when the surprise clears, I see he looks a little hurt.

"Jae, I'm sorry I was so rude," I say, trying to catch my breath at the same time.

He shrugs. "What'd I do?" He looks so little-boyish, all of a sudden I have a mad urge to hug him. I don't. I take a deep breath instead.

"You kissed me when you already had a girlfriend," I say, then wait for the sky to fall.

"Huh?" Another confused look passes over him. "Ellen, I don't have a girlfriend."

I pause a few seconds, then scrutinize his face as a jeweler does a gem, trying to determine his authenticity.

"Um, someone in tae kwon do said that's probably why you don't come to class on Fridays," I say, not wanting to drag Sookie into this.

Jae explodes with laughter. "Who was it? Ralph? Sookie? My Fridays are considerably less romantic than that."

My face is flaring in embarrassment.

"So do you want to study Korean now?" Jae says, his grin returning tentatively.

I put out my hand, and he takes it.

At Weld, we pass up the study lounge. "Want to do it in my room?" Jae asks.

"Study," I say.

"Of course," he says.

Jae's roommate, Charlie, is hanging out in the common room when we get there, so we go into the bedroom.

"Let me guess which is your side," I say. At one end of the small room the walls are plastered with posters of the Celtics, St. Pauli Girl beer ("You never forget your first Girl"), and Cindy Crawford. The bed, with a wrinkled Mexican blanket thrown over it, is home to a pair of sneakers, a squash racquet, books, and a Walkman.

The other side is completely bare: blank walls, a bed with

a gray blanket covering it. The desk is clear except for two framed pictures and a pencil holder.

"Is this your family?" I say, reaching for a picture that encompasses several generations. In the back, an elderly woman in traditional dress presides over several couples with softer, smiling faces. In the very front are a bunch of mischievous-looking kids: a girl in pink and green palm-tree sunglasses; a boy — Jae, I'd bet — with a tooth missing; and a few toddlers with Jae's eyes.

"Uh-huh," Jae says, leaning over me to point. "This is my *halmoni*, my grandmother. This is my uncle — Dad's brother — and aunt. These are my parents, my cousins, me."

He puts the picture gently back, and we study diligently for about an hour, Jae correcting me as I read aloud. Then he gets out some wine from a TV-sized fridge.

"So why *don't* you show up for tae kwon do on Fridays?" I ask him.

"I work," Jae says.

"Schoolwork work?" I ask.

"No, work work," he says. "For Harvard Security."

He gets up, opens an immaculately ordered closet (one Michelle would love), and extracts a gray workshirt. HARVARD SECURITY says the badge on the arm. The name embroidered on the front is "Jay."

"So what do you do?"

"Wander around the Science Center at night and make sure no criminals get in."

"And how often do you go?"

"Fridays, Tuesdays, Thursdays, and whenever else they need."

"How do you find the time to study?"

"Are you from the Child Labor Board or something?"

"I'm sorry," I say. "I didn't mean to pry. It's just that with all the schoolwork they give us here, I don't know how you have the time to do it. Can you study on the job?"

"Not really," Jae says. "We have to keep moving and radio in from various checkpoints. It's not too strenuous, though."

"I think even if I wanted to, my parents wouldn't let me get a job while I'm here," I tell him. "They're really into this 'studying comes first' business."

Jae smiles, a bit wryly, I think.

"My parents don't know I have a job," he says. "I work because my aunt and uncle are supporting me, and I want to help them out any way I can."

What about his parents? I wonder. The look on his face reminds me of the time he told me about going to see Irwin.

"Does this have anything to do with how you were feeling sad at the beginning of the semester?"

Jae nods slowly.

"Do you want to talk about it?"

Jae sits there for a moment. "The riots," he says finally. The words seem bottled up inside him. "The ones in L.A. Remember them?"

"Of course I do," I say. "Even in Arkin, Minnesota, they were big news on TV."

"My parents' store was destroyed."

Silence. Invisible hands seem to be squeezing the beats out of my heart.

"Jae, I'm sorry," I say finally. Why did I assume his father was a doctor, like mine?

"Don't feel sorry for me," Jae says. "A lot of people went through much worse. A Korean guy only a little older than me was killed. But you asked; now you know."

"Your parents," I say. "Are they okay?"

"Thank God, yeah, but . . ." His jaw sets. There is a slight tremor underneath.

"But what?"

"They went back to Korea," he says, looking away. "They tried to rebuild, but they couldn't, in the end. Their hearts were broken."

"Oh, Jae," I say. I think to myself, how can this person keep so much inside him? If my parents moved back to Korea, I don't think I would be able to stand it.

I gingerly put a hand on his back. His muscles harden under my touch.

Control, I think. He's perfectly in control.

It's funny how easily you can fall into believing you have a person all figured out when you haven't even scratched the surface. Here I was so quick to believe that Jae was a sleazy two-timer.

Jae doesn't kiss me when he drops me off at my room. This leaves me in a state of half relief, half agitation.

Relationships are all about building bridges. Sturdy bridges take time.

"You look like you're messed up, girl!" Leecia says when I walk in the door.

"Don't ask," I say, heading to the privacy of the bedroom.

Chapter Fifteen

I SHOW UP at the appointed time at Marianne Stoeller's office, my knees quaking. The last time I felt this sick with dread was at my Harvard interview last year. The lilac-scarf girl (to be fair, I know her name is Suzanne) told me everything I needed to know in the last class, so why should I have to go through it again?

"Come in," Marianne Stoeller says.

I step into her office, which is floor-to-ceiling books. By that I mean books on the floor, books on the desk, books stacked high to the ceiling. There is just enough clear space to get to a chair that has graciously been kept book-free.

Marianne Stoeller sits at her desk. She is holding a clay mug of coffee in her hands. On her fourth finger is a silver ring that's so big it looks masculine.

"So how are you liking the class?" she asks kindly.

"I like it a lot," I answer honestly.

"Good." She seems genuinely delighted. She takes a moment to sift through some folders, then I notice that my "home" piece and all my other assignments are spread out like an exposed poker hand on her desk.

"You'll see that my comments are pretty vague, because this is just the 'feely' part of the course. After you write some more stories, my criticisms will become more specific."

The dreaded "Coming Up Roses" is sitting in front of her nose. When is she going to say something about it?

"So far," she says, surveying the assignments, taking a sip of coffee, and smiling, "I think you're doing just fine."

"Whh-at?" I say, almost falling out of my chair. I recover my politeness at least: "Excuse me?" I say.

"Your 'home' piece was quite original, and I liked the characters in 'Like Father, Like Daughter.' "

"But everyone hated 'Coming Up Roses,' " I protest.

"No one *hated* it, Ellen," she says. "I think the point that was made is that you were trying to write like Flannery O'Connor when you should be trying to write like Ellen Sung. There's nothing wrong with studying the masters, but when it comes to writing, you must have the courage to let your own voice emerge."

There is a knock on the door, and Suzanne of the lilac scarf sticks her head in.

"I'm here," she says to Marianne Stoeller.

"Good," she says, smiling. "We're not quite finished, so would you please shut the door?"

Marianne Stoeller is so much like her own stories: gentle and loving surface, yet at the core a sure hand that cuts through dross.

"Ellen, I think your voice comes through clearest in 'Like Father, Like Daughter.' That narrative has a certain authenticity to it."

"Do you think so?" I say, then admit, "I was ready to give
up for a while there."

"Nothing worth doing comes easily," Marianne Stoeller says. "I know it sounds corny, but it's very true. Especially with writing. It wasn't easy for Flannery O'Connor, or Hemingway, or me, or anybody. You just have to keep writing."

Keep writing, I think. That's it: I need practice. So I guess it's okay that I don't write about Greek myth.

Later, as I walk away from Marianne Stoeller's office, I feel a different kind of trembling inside me. A story is rumbling, asking to be let out. I recognize the signs this time.

I rush back to Weld. Leecia has classes all afternoon so I know I'll have the place to myself until four. I've hardly shaken off my coat before I'm at my desk. I scribble "Jessie's Pride" at the top of a piece of paper. I've been thinking a lot about Jessie and about Arkin lately, and with this wonderful bit of encouragement from Marianne Stoeller, I think I'm ready to write.

I'm so excited about this story, I don't even bother to change any names.

*

On Sundays, Leecia and I have fallen into the nicest routine: one of us goes out and buys the *New York Times*, fresh juice, and croissants. Then we sit in our room and read all morning, no matter how much work we have. It's routines like this that keep me sane. And it's good to keep up with what's going on in the world, even though I admittedly sometimes skip world-news articles for the style section.

"Who are you voting for, Leecia, if I may ask?" I say, reminding myself to turn in my absentee ballot. I obviously don't want to miss out on my first presidential election.

"No one," she says.

"Ha-ha," I say.

"No," she says, "I'm serious. I'm not voting for anyone. If Jesse's not running, I'm not voting."

"You're kidding," I say.

"Nope. None of the clowns on the ballot cares at all about black folks, so I'm protesting by not voting."

"But Leecia," I say, "your vote will be wasted."

"Not wasted — conserved," she says. "I'm sick of how the Democrats assume they'll get our vote just because they're not Republicans. They totally avoided black issues in the campaign — those smug jerks."

"I agree," I say. "But someone's going to get elected. So maybe none of them has a good civil rights record, but how about other issues? You're pro-choice, so why not vote for the pro-choice candidate?"

"Those issues aren't as important to me as representation by people of my color," Leecia says.

"What? Are you saying you're black before you're a woman? What would happen if I decided not to vote until there was an Asian American candidate for president?"

"That would be your choice," Leecia says.

But voting is a privilege, a freedom. If everyone acted like you did, I'm about to say, *no one would vote and democracy would die!* But then Monica knocks on our door.

"Anyone up for brunch at the Union?" she asks.

"No thanks," Leecia says. "But we have plenty of croissants here if you want to join us."

"And we can make more coffee," I add. Monica looks delighted and proceeds to join our kaffeeklatsch. We start talking about something else.

Later, I find myself wishing I had made my point on voting more forcefully to Leecia, shown her how important the right to vote is. But who am I to think *she's* wrong? She has her own reasons, and I should respect them.

Chapter Sixteen

THE NEXT THING I know it's Thanksgiving and I'm on an Amtrak train bound for Baltimore with Leecia and Monica.

"This is going to be such a blast," Leecia exhorts as we settle into our seats. "I have a billion friends who are dying to meet you, Ellen."

Monica drags out her big *Cell* book and puts it on her lap. I stare at her with premed guilt for a minute, then throw my bags, books and all, in the overhead rack. It's vacation, right?

"What's Jae doing for Thanksgiving?" Leecia asks.

"He's going to New York with some friends," I say. In some ways I regret that the Thanksgiving break has inserted itself like this. Jae and I have been wanting to spend time together, but in the last week, with his work schedule and his KASH meetings, it's been impossible. I'm kind of curious now to know what goes on at KASH, since Jae seems so devoted to it.

The train pulls out with a lurch.

"The major cities we'll be passing through," Leecia says,

sounding like a conductor, "are Providence, home of Brown University; New Haven, home of Yale; New York, home of Columbia; and Balto, home of Leecia and Monica."

Monica, already immersed in her *Cell* book, doesn't look up. I wish I had her concentration, but this trip is so exciting. I've never been on a train before; in Minnesota, people drive everywhere.

It has turned dark by the time Leecia's mom picks us up at the station. After dropping Monica off, we go to their house, which is a colonial, and it's huge. The kitchen is twice the size of ours in Arkin, and all the appliances are white and brand-spanking new.

"We just had it redone," Mrs. Thomas says, probably noting my admiringly open mouth. She makes us hot chocolate from scratch, whipping it up in a flurry but somehow not messing up the tailored navy suit she's wearing.

"Any exciting cases today?" Leecia asks, beginning to lap up her hot chocolate.

"My only excitement was picking you girls up," her mom answers. Then she turns to me. "The bad thing about being a real estate lawyer is that the cases are so dull."

"Bet you'd love to get your hands on a gory murder case," I say.

"Absolutely," she says, giving me exactly Leecia's mischievous look.

"But at least you get to come home at a reasonable hour," Leecia says, making a face. "Not like Dad."

Leecia's father is an executive at a company called Technotron, which manufactures some kind of part for video terminals.

He still isn't home by seven, when we begin dinner.

Leecia's grandma has returned with Leecia's little brother and sister from some after-school activity, and we all sit down to eat. I guess because I'm a guest, we eat in the dining room, which has a beautiful chandelier over the table. On one wall, a portrait of Martin Luther King, Jr. watches us benevolently.

That night, Leecia and I prepare to sleep in one room as we do in school. Leecia drags out a fold-out cot, puts some bedding on it, then plops down with her nighttime reading.

"Leecia," I say, "wouldn't you like to sleep in your own bed?"

"Don't be silly," she says. "You're a guest."

"You're silly," I say. "You're home. It's your bed. It doesn't matter to me where I sleep."

Leecia is adamant, however, so I end up in her Scandinavian-style oak bed. The mattress is firm, almost hard — just the way I like it.

*

The Thomases do their best to make me feel at home. I brought a fruit basket as a present, and they oohed and ahed over it as if they'd never seen one before.

On Thanksgiving, I meet a bunch of their friends and relatives. The Thanksgiving meal is conducted around a huge table groaning with food — Mrs. Thomas uses a bunch of leaves to extend their regular dining room table — with tons of people of all ages, and kids running around. Very Norman Rockwellesque.

Our Thanksgivings in Arkin have always been just us. We don't have any relatives in the U.S. except for a very removed cousin of Father's who supposedly lives in Amarillo. I wonder what it'd be like to have such a lively home.

After the meal I make sure to call Mom and Father.

In the next few days, Leecia and I go Christmas shopping at a beautiful marketplace by the harbor, and we meet with her friends at night. The Friday after Thanksgiving we stay out until three in the morning. In Arkin, this used to be the vacation's biggest party night. I wonder what Jessie is doing this year.

On our last day, I use the Thomases' nice big yard to practice my tae kwon do forms, since the test is coming up in a few weeks. I wonder if the Thomases think I'm a nut, high kicking and *kihaping* at no one in particular. Leecia's little brother and sister stay out to watch me and don't say a word.

For dinner that night, Leecia's grandma makes us a huge meal of ribs, gumbo, greens, blackeyed peas, and even sweet potato pie that has marshmallows on top of it — delicious.

"Gran's from the South," Leecia says as we push away from the table, as bloated as two whales. "Mom's a Yankee. They cook equally well, but I think I might like southern food a little better."

"I have never eaten anything this good in my life," I say.

We return to campus rested from being so pampered. I'm a little surprised at how well the visit went. Usually, I'm not one hundred percent comfortable staying in other people's homes, but for some reason I just slid in and settled with the Thomases.

When we return to the suite, there's a message from Jae saying he wants to see *Love Story* with me.

Chapter Seventeen

"S o do you want to see the movie?" Jae asks when I call back. "After all, it's set at Harvard."

"I know — I read the book," I say. "I think it might be really sappy."

"Everyone should see *Love Story* at least once while living here," Leecia calls from the common room. "Preferably with someone you have the hots for."

"Okay, okay," I say, trying to cover the phone's mouthpiece too late. "Want to come pick me up, Jae?"

Jae shows up in a faded denim shirt, Levi's, no baseball cap.

"My, don't you look spiffy," Leecia says, looking him up and down.

Jae blushes. I think he *has* gotten a little dressed up for me, and I feel touched.

"I won't keep her out too late," he promises in mock politeness.

We leave Leecia to her studying and go to Mem Hall, where *Love Story* is playing. The movie turns out to be incredibly maudlin. But still, when Ali McGraw dies of cancer, I cry.

"Oh, Ellen," Jae says as he squeezes my hand.

"I guess I'd better not go into oncology," I say damply, throwing a small pile of used tissues into a trash bin.

After ice cream, we go back to Weld. Leecia is still dressed, not in her pajamas as I would have expected.

"Monica rented an Eddie Murphy movie for her VCR," she says, grabbing a tote bag. "I'm going over there to watch. See you in the morning."

"In the morning?" I say.

"Yeah. I'll be too tired to come back, and she said I can stay over."

I look at Leecia; I know what she's up to.

"Don't leave because of us," Jae says, before I do.

"Don't be silly," she answers. "I love Eddie Murphy."

"Leecia," I say.

"See you!" She glides out the door before we can stop her.

Leecia's footsteps fade down the hall, then all is quiet. Alone at last. I've been wanting this, but now that it's here, my nerves are tied in softball-sized knots. And how does Jae feel?

"Wellll . . . " Jae says, taking my hand.

We end up piled on my narrow bed. Jae is on top, heavy like our breathing. From zero to sixty in less than ten seconds — too fast. I'm wildly attracted to him, and my body is doing things without asking permission from my brain.

"I'm a virgin," I manage to say before his mouth descends like a ton of bricks.

"I think you'd better stay that way for a while," he says,

not missing a beat. "Like me."

I am so surprised I sit up on one elbow. All motion stops, settles — a top suddenly winding down.

"You're a *virgin?*" I say, looking at him as if he were a specimen preserved in formaldehyde.

"It's true. Now, do I look like an Asian geek to you, or what?"

"I wish you'd quit saying that," I say. "The reason I'm so surprised is that all the guys I know seem to want to throw away their virginity as soon as possible. And you're so nice-looking."

Jae seems to relax a little bit, although his chest is still heaving. I resist the urge to touch him again. My hormones, or something, are out of control.

"I want to make love to you so bad," he says. "But I know better."

"This is too fast," I agree, remembering the lectures we had during freshman week: how to use condoms, the staggering statistics on AIDS and other STDs. The football players acted like it was a big joke. I have to admit I didn't take it too seriously either. I wasn't going to have sex with someone for a *long* while, I remember thinking at the time. So how did I go from fiercely guarded virginity to this?

Now is not the time to be sorting this stuff out.

"Let's sleep," I suggest, although I doubt I can.

Jae and I curl up against each other, our bodies fitting closely together like spoons.

I'm never going to get to sleep this way, I think, my whole body abuzz with being so close to him, his mouth so close to the back of my neck.

But to my surprise, when I open my eyes, it's morning.

Chapter Eighteen

O N THE DAY of my tae kwon do test, I'm wildly nervous. I've had plenty of help from Jae and Sookie, in class and out, but I'm still a mess — I really want this belt. After getting my yellow belt I'll still be considered a beginner, but there's something so enticing about having a *colored* belt.

"I wish you were testing with me," I say to Jae as we eat lunch together with Leecia. He'll be taking a special black-belt test in the spring.

"Don't worry, I'll be there to watch you."

"You'll do great, Ellen," Leecia says. "And when you're done and I'm back from my Alliance meeting, we'll celebrate."

That night, the wrestling room is buzzing. The people who are testing plus the black belts are the only ones in uniform. I see Jae out of the corner of my eye; he is smiling at me.

Ralph leads us through warmups, then Master Han sits down in the front with a clipboard in his hands. My heart starts to race and I try to regulate my breathing, as we've been taught, to relax myself.

We white belts go first. There are four guys and me in the first group. Ralph calls out each of our names and has us stand on one of several masking-tape X's on the floor. To my dismay, I'm put right up front.

We go through our white-belt forms, then show off our prearranged self-defense techniques. While breaking a stranglehold, I trip over my partner's foot, but luckily, Master Han is looking farther down the line.

The last part of the test is the one I dread the most: breaking boards.

The black belts get up to hold the boards. Sookie holds mine. "Don't worry," she whispers to me, looking at my face. "This is the easiest part."

She holds the board in front of her with her elbows locked. We're supposed to step in and break the board with a simple side kick. Sounds easy, except that it's a *board*, and boards are hard — harder than my foot, I imagine.

I should have had Jae switch my board with a balsa wood one, or one of those prebroken trick ones they use in movies. Now, why didn't I think of that earlier?

Master Han tells us to get into our ready stances, and before I know it, he says *sijak*, which means go, and all of us step toward the board-holders and fire away. I pray I won't kick Sookie's hand.

My foot meets the board, goes through it. Sookie is holding two halves of scrap lumber.

My first thought is *Jae, that son of a gun, really did switch the boards for me!*

With a wink, Sookie hands me the splintered pieces. They are real.

"Congratulations," says Master Han. He hands each of us a saffron-colored belt. We testees all bow gratefully.

*

Back at Weld, Leecia has two kinds of tea waiting, plus Mint Milano cookies — my favorite.

"I knew you'd do great," she says.

Chapter Nineteen

"YOU NEVER DID tell me why Jae was never at tae kwon do on Fridays," Leecia says to me as we're drinking coffee in a grungy diner an appreciable way off campus.

"He works," I tell her. "For Harvard Security."

"He works?" Leecia says. "You're kidding."

"I don't know how he finds the time, either."

"Oh, that's not what surprises me," Leecia says. "I always think of Korean students as being rich."

"Really," I say. "Why?"

"Oh, I don't know, I just do," Leecia says. "Maybe it's because you guys are always dressed so nice or something."

"Leecia," I say, staring at her over my worn china cup, "Jae's family lost their store, and pretty much all their assets, in the L.A. riots."

"Oh." Leecia takes in a breath sharply.

"I know he seems cheerful," I say. "But he's working his tail off at that job. I guess his aunt and uncle are helping to put him through school."

"Wow, I really admire him for that," Leecia says. "He never complains. Was he there at the riots?"

"I think so," I say. "He's slowly filling me in on the details."

"Here we are at Harvard," Leecia says, "and we might know someone who was actually there at the riots."

I find it hard to believe sometimes, too. At home we had watched the post-riot TV interviews of the Korean storekeepers, recounting their stories in halting English. Father had remarked, "You know, the Koreans in Koreatown are nothing like us."

When I asked what he meant, he said, "When your mother and I came to America in 1959, it was very difficult for Koreans to enter this country. They only took the best, the most educated. Your mother and I spoke good English before we even left Korea. Now, things are different. Anyone can come in, open a store, and become rich, without learning much English! We are nothing like those immigrants."

At the time, watching the Korean storeowners on TV — especially the thuglike ones shooting guns from military stances — I remember thinking, *Yes, Father's right, these people are not like us at all.*

But now, knowing Jae, the kaleidoscope of my perspective is slowly changing. His parents must be pretty smart to have a son who can get into Harvard. And Jae speaks both English and Korean — one up on me.

"Maybe it's not the case with Jae's family," Leecia says. "But I heard that Koreans make lots of money off those small stores, especially liquor stores."

"I have no idea," I say. "I did hear my father complaining once about how Koreans these days can just come over to the the U.S., open a store, and get rich quick. But poor Jae! I think his work takes a lot out of him."

"He'd be a hard worker no matter what kind of background he came from," Leecia says. "He's a great guy — hang on to him."

"I'll try," I promise.

"Can I ask you something?"

"Sure," I say.

Leecia leans forward, gently pushes a swath of my hair away, and looks at my face intently. "Where did you get those scars?"

"From a girl," I say.

"Want to tell me about it?"

"Yes," I say. "I always meant to. There was this girl at my high school; her name was Marsha Randall. She hated me for some reason, and really, really liked my boyfriend, Tomper."

"A recipe for disaster already," Leecia remarks.

"She was the captain of the gymnastics team, which I was on, and she used to make my life miserable by calling me all those wonderful names people have for Asians. She'd do it in the open, too, and the coach would pretend she didn't hear."

"No way!"

"Yup. I dealt with it in my own passive way, trying to ignore her, all that. I even tried to befriend her once."

"So what happened?" Leecia says, her eyes wide.

"At a party at the end of the year, she said something to

me and shoved me around, so I punched her. Then she came after me with a broken bottle, and I sort of stopped it with my face. Too bad I didn't know tae kwon do then."

"Oh, my God!" Leecia says. "Did she go to jail?"

"I ended up not pressing charges." I shrug. "It was one of those weird things where I knew she wasn't going to change, jail or no jail, and I guess I felt a tiny bit sorry for her because her racism was almost like a sickness. Maybe I took the wimp's way out, not wanting to deal with all the court stuff right before school. I still don't know."

"You had your reasons," Leecia says. "But your scars aren't very noticeable at all. It's only when you pull your hair back to wash your face that I can even see them."

"My dad, who's a doctor, said he thought the healing was pretty good, considering the damage that had been done. Maybe God decided I did a good thing. Then again, maybe it was because my friends got me to the hospital right away."

"Can't beat good friends," Leecia says, her eyes sparking behind her coffee cup.

"That's for sure," I say.

Chapter Twenty

W HEN MICHELLE AND I head home for Christmas, our luggage contains more books than clothes or presents. Harvard, for some archaic reason, holds its final exams after the Christmas break instead of before, like the other Ivy League schools. Thus, for the past two years I've had to endure holidays watching Michelle study and stress out. This year I'll join her.

The extent of the Christmas spirit in my dorm room was a poinsettia plant Leecia and I purchased at Store 24, and we both guessed that it would probably die over break. We exchanged quick gifts before we left, Leecia giving me a sleek black fountain pen, almost too beautiful to use, and me giving her a James Baldwin first edition that I'd found in an antiquarian bookstore in Boston.

As for Jae, I wasn't sure if we were at the gift-giving stage yet. I bought, but didn't give him, a leather-bound notebook, because he'd mentioned how he'd like to start keeping a journal.

"*Anyonghaseo,*" I immediately say to Mom and Father when they pick Michelle and me up at the airport.

"Myong-Ok," Mom says with delight, "where did you learn that?"

"From a friend of mine at school," I say, then add unnecessarily, "He's Korean."

There is a message from Jessie waiting for me when we get back to the house. I dump my stuff in my room — *my room* — and then rush to talk to her. I'm so hyper, it feels as though I'm back in high school again — as though I've just spent the weekend away and now I need to call Jessie to catch up on everything I missed.

*

"This is just like old times," Jessie says to me over a Polar Burger and fries at the Northern Lights Saloon. It seems like all our high school friends are here, eating in the restaurant or hanging out at the connected bar/dance hall.

"Ellen, I somehow expected you to look different, but you look the same."

"It's only been four months," I say, although Jessie herself has a new, shorter hair style and she's wearing more eye makeup than she used to.

"Well, I thought you might get Harvard tattooed on your forehead or something," she says. "Mike said he thought you'd look all fancy."

"All fancy, Jessie?" I roll my eyes. "Dream on."

"Ever hear from Tomper?" she asks.

"Once." Guilt gently pokes at my stomach. "I wrote him but haven't heard since. He sounded kind of lonesome."

"Yeah, boot camp, that must be pretty rough," she says. "He's such a nice guy. But I guess you must be meeting lots of guys at Harvard."

"I've met one," I say. "The Jae I mentioned before. And that's enough."

"Oh, you're still seeing that guy? That's good."

After we eat, Jessie and I hang out in the dance room. A local band, Custer's Last Stand, is playing tonight. The music is purely country, which everyone *hated* in high school, and I'm amazed to see tons of my former classmates getting up to dance in a line. I even see Kent Norvald and Dan Janssen, guys too macho even to be seen dancing at prom, up there, knowing all the steps.

"When did country get so big here, Jessie?" I ask.

"You mean it's not big out East?" Jessie says with incredulity. "What about Lenny Skaggins, or Houston Brooks?"

"I've heard of them," I say. "But I guess at Harvard people are into more alternative stuff, like the Sonic Booms and the Remainders."

"Hmm," Jessie says suspiciously. Then she pulls me into the line. "You've got to take some real midwestern culture back with you," she insists.

I look down at everyone's feet, trying to get a grip on the different hoedown steps. Dan Janssen is actually wearing cowboy boots — he wouldn't have been caught dead in them in high school. How could things have changed so quickly?

"Hey, Ellen!" Dan yells. "How are things at Yale?"

I wave back and nod, pretending that it's too much trouble to talk over the music.

Jessie and I do the country two-step until one, when the lights turn on full in our faces — our hint to leave.

"Want to cruise?" Jessie asks as we slip into her cold-as-a-coffin car. Our breath rises in semisolid wisps around the pine-tree–shaped air freshener hanging from the rearview mirror.

"Yeah, let's go," I say, shivering slightly. The night is young, and for once I don't have to worry about a curfew.

Jessie drives the usual loop: up Main, past the hardware store, and back again. Once, in high school, we cruised around for so long we actually had to stop and get gas.

"So how's work?" I ask. Jessie had mentioned in one of her letters that she'd finally gotten a job, as a secretary for Sklaarg Insurance in Arkin.

"Boring," she says.

"What do you do there?"

"Type a lot of shit and file, mostly," she says, lighting up a cigarette. I've always marveled at her ability to smoke and drive a stick shift at the same time.

"Why didn't you go to Duluth with Mike?"

"Lord knows I wanted to," she says. "But I couldn't leave my dad."

"But you're a high school graduate," I say gently. "I think your dad will survive."

Jessie's mom died when Jessie was twelve, and since then she's been the one running everything at their house.

"His liver's getting worse, and it's screwing him up at work," she answers flatly.

"Well, can he retire soon?" I ask, trying to be delicate. The reason her father has such problems with his liver is that he drinks a lot.

"He's got to hang in there if he's going to get his pension," Jessie says. "I know he *looks* old, but he's got quite a few birthdays to pass before Arkin Taconite will give him what he deserves."

I am listening to Jessie, as I always do, but I notice I am also mentally recording details: the wrinkle that seems to be etching itself on one side of her mouth, the way her voice tightens when she talks about her father. It seems these images are passing through my mind and mutating into scenes for my story "Jessie's Pride."

"What I don't know," Jessie says, sighing, "is who'll take care of him when I get married."

"Married?" I gulp. "You aren't planning to do that soon, are you?"

Jessie turns to me. "I know Mike is the one . . . so what's the use of delaying anything? He always says I'm the person he wants to spend the rest of his life with. I have a feeling I'll get a ring for Christmas."

"No way, Jess, you're kidding," I say. "I mean, you're young."

"And getting older," Jessie says.

"But aren't you going to start taking classes at the community college?" I ask gently, hopefully. "Jessie, you're so smart."

"Smart is one thing," she says. "But to go to college, you need money. Mike will be the one to go. I'll do fine with an MRS degree. Who needs college if all I'm going to do is stay home with the kids?"

"Stay home with the kids?" I involuntarily echo. "But your music —"

"We sold the piano." Jessie's voice has a cold, adultlike

tone to it that is jarring. "Ellen, get real. There's no way I was going to become a concert pianist, and I'm certainly not going to start Jessie's School of Music for Bratty Kids."

What am I doing at college? I think wildly. Jessie should be the one to go.

"You know, about my dad," she says thoughtfully. "I wonder if he started drinking in high school, like we did. I saw in his yearbook he was voted best dancer or something, so he must have been pretty popular."

I try to think of Jessie's dad: florid, large, balding. It's hard to think of him as a high school charmer. But who knows what *we'll* look like twenty years hence?

"I've figured out that at some point, alcohol turns from your friend to your enemy," she says. "I just have to figure out when that point is."

"And quit before it," I add.

We pass Hardee's, the only thing on the strip that's open at this hour. Inside we can see high school kids in their Arkin High jackets. They're probably gossiping about who's sharing french fries with whom. Maybe some of them are the big seniors who rule the school, just like we used to think we did.

I remember those dark nights, just Jessie and me. We used to think life would always be a cruise: driving around, trying to spot the guys we liked. I even used to think that a song on the radio could hold all the secrets to life, the luminous dials of the radio a mysterious, glowing Buddha in the dark. A cute boyfriend was all I thought I needed.

When did life change? When did I realize I had to stop deluding myself, thinking that Mom and Father would be around forever, to take care of me forever, and that life would take care of itself? I guess it must have to do with being at college: I no longer see them every day, and if I ever needed to, running to the safety of home is now more difficult. I like being more on my own, but it's scary, too. I wonder if that's one reason why Jessie wants to hurry up and get married.

"Do you ever miss high school, Jessie?" I ask.

"Yeah, lots," she says without hesitation. "Things were so much simpler then."

Chapter Twenty-One

"THERE'S A PACKAGE waiting for you at the post office," Mom says, showing me a little yellow piece of paper — certified mail.

The return address says Boston.

I feel like going for a walk, so I put on my snow boots and tramp out to the post office. There I exchange the yellow slip for a small package. It's from Jae.

In my room, door shut, I cut through the tape very carefully. The brown paper wrapping falls away to reveal a simple but cleverly crafted wooden box. I open it. On a mat of cotton is a pale green pendant shaped like a half-moon, heavy-looking, attached to a velvet cord.

I pick it up. It's not a stone but cool porcelain — a mysterious, beautiful pale green. I put it on.

*

"Where did you get that?" Father asks, peering at my present during dinner.

"From a friend of mine at school."

Father scrutinizes it closely. "Do you know what it is?"

"A pendant?" I say.

"It's celadon," he says, and then he looks at Mom. "It looks like a really old piece." Mom nods.

"What's celadon?" I ask.

"It's a kind of Korean pottery," Father says. "This shade of green is very special — our family used to have a few pieces like that back in Korea."

"Are you still seeing that Jae guy?" Michelle asks. "I thought you were just studying Korean with him."

"Are you dating a Korean boy?" Mom asks, her curiosity antennae perking up.

"We're not really dating," I say.

"But he is Korean, right?" Mom says, smiling. I nod.

"What does his father do?" Father asks.

I take a bite of my tuna casserole. "His parents are merchants; they owned a grocery." Then I add, "It was destroyed in the L.A. riots."

Father looks thoughtful. We eat on in temporary silence.

"That is such a shame," Father says, shaking his head. "Those blacks, they are such bad people. The Koreans work hard, and for what? Those people are just jealous."

"Father!" I say, a little more sharply than I meant to.

"They are lazy," Father continues. "They get mad when they see the Koreans working so hard."

"Father, that's not quite fair," I say. "My roommate is black, and she works even harder than I do."

"Leecia is black?" Mom says with surprise. "She doesn't sound black over the phone."

"Not all blacks sound like the Jeffersons on TV." I sigh, but I suddenly realize that the only contact my parents have with blacks *is* via the TV.

"Ellen's right," Michelle says. "It doesn't do anyone any
good to generalize about people by race."

Father suddenly stops chewing and looks at Michelle, then at me. I don't think he's used to us being home, talking back to him. When we were little, he was always saying, "If we were in Korea you would not be talking to me like this." I always wondered what things were like in Korea because we were always *very* respectful — much more respectful than my friends were to their parents. Maybe now that I'm in college, I'm becoming more opinionated. But isn't that what college is for — to learn how to think objectively?

"Anyway, Ellen, if your friend is the son of a Korean grocer," Father says, "ask him where he got the money to buy a pendant like that. A piece that old would cost a lot of money."

"I will," I say, inwardly chastising myself for wearing the thing and starting this whole mess. First my parents disapproved of Tomper, because he wasn't exactly college material. But now that I've gone off to Harvard and found a college boy — a *Korean* one at that — to them, he's just the son of a Koreatown grocer.

*

"I got it!" Jessie yells at me over the phone. "The most beautiful engagement ring in the whole world."

"No way!"

"You won't believe how he did it either," Jessie says. "The present he put under the tree was in this huge box, one you might stick a deluxe box of Lincoln Logs in, so naturally I was pretty disappointed — and I told him so! Poor guy — I was such a crab to him all week."

"Then what?"

"Then Christmas Eve he was over, and I opened the package. It was heavy because he'd weighted it with all these old hockey pucks. And inside was a teeny box."

"So clever and romantic," I remark.

"And of course it was a diamond ring when I opened it — a marquise setting, my favorite."

"Oh, wow, Jessie," I say.

"Then he even got down on one knee and proposed. I was bawling by then."

"Oh, wow, Jessie," I say again, different emotions mixing themselves in a salad in my stomach. I'm happy, envious, apprehensive. On one hand, Jessie suddenly seems so grown up, getting married and starting a family. On the other, it seems like she and Mike are two kids playing house. At our age, what could they, or anyone, possibly know about life?

"That's so great," I say. "So when's the big day?"

"Probably next fall sometime," she says. "You'll be my maid of honor, right?"

"Of course, of course," I say.

"Just think, I'm going to be Mrs. Michael Anderson," Jessie says.

*

I call Jae just before it's time to go back. I had sent his present by priority mail the day after I received mine.

"Hey, Ellen!" His voice seems to light up the phone wires. "Thanks so much for the great gift — I've started writing in it already."

"And your gift. . . . "

"It's celadon, a kind of Korean pottery," he says.

"I know. My parents told me all about it. In fact, they said it's really expensive."

"That pendant belonged to my grandmother," Jae says. "When she died, it was given to me, since there aren't any girls in our family."

"Then it's priceless," I say uneasily.

"It's for you," Jae says. "This might sound a little weird, but the first day I saw you in Weld, I thought of how good the pendant would look on you."

"Jae," I challenge, "I bet you can't actually remember the first day we met."

"Believe what you want to believe." Jae laughs. "I remember that day — you were so cute, trying to lug those suitcases up the stairs."

"I guess you do remember."

"Of course I do," he says. "I love you, Ellen."

The words hit me, even though they're just transmissions over the wires.

I love Jae-Chun Kim, too, I realize. Now what do I do?

Chapter Twenty-Two

O N THE PLANE back to school, Michelle upsets the flight attendant by refusing to put her tray table up.

"We can't take off until your tray table is in its upright position," the woman says, biting her lip nervously. She is wearing pink lipstick and a lot of blue eyeshadow. She doesn't look any older than Michelle.

I feel sorry for her, so I give Michelle a warning nudge in her ribs. She reluctantly sweeps off her books and notebooks and puts the plastic table up with a sigh. "I don't see what the big deal is," she says, looking the flight attendant in the eye. "If we crash, we'll all burn up and die anyway."

Michelle is her normal pre-exam self. On the way to the airport, she complained the whole time that she hadn't gotten enough studying in. Mom and Father are used to this behavior and didn't take it personally. For me, it makes me wonder if I should be studying harder. But how can I be?

*

Reading period is a time to study for finals or catch up on the stuff you blew off all semester, depending on what kind of student you are. Luckily, I have kept up on my work, and my short stories class turned out to be a boon because I finished my final project, twenty pages of stories, at home.

In fact, home is where I finished up "Jessie's Pride," which turned into the story of a girl who loses her mother early on in life. She ends up marrying young to establish her independence from her loving but very needy father. This story, plus a couple of entirely new ones, are part of a collection of what I call my Arkin stories.

So basically, for my finals, I just have to go over all my chem, bio, and math notes ad nauseam. Most Harvard extracurriculars, such as tae kwon do, are suspended during this time, and I barely see Jae. He is still working for Harvard Security, even though he's taking a lot of hard classes, including physics, which I hear is particularly brutal.

"Are you sure you can't get someone else to take over for you?" I ask him one day after a hurried dinner together. He is beginning to look haggard from lack of sleep.

"Ellen, it's not just the work," he says. "I need the money. My cousins are reaching college age, and my aunt and uncle certainly are not rich."

"What do they do?" I ask.

"They own a grocery in Boston," he says.

"Runs in the family, huh?" I say.

"I guess," Jae says. "A grocery is a logical place to start, especially when employers aren't dying to hire an immigrant who doesn't speak English well."

We get to his suite and go in. Jae puts on his work clothes.

"Are you sure you have to go?" I ask. "Couldn't you call

in sick just once so you could get some rest?" I admit I'm a little frightened by the way his usual vitality seems to have been bleached out of his face.

"Ellen," he says, putting his hands on my shoulders, "in life, there are things you just have to do."

He then leaves me to spend the night walking through dark and empty corridors.

Chapter Twenty-Three

I END THE SEMESTER with two A's and two B's. Leecia ends it with three A's and one B. I was surprised and disappointed by my B in bio, my best subject in high school. However, I got an A in chem by the skin of my teeth — two points. I am forever grateful to Michelle for telling me to fight for my points in lab: they were the ones that made the difference.

My other A was in short stories. I couldn't believe my eyes when I picked up my portfolio and saw the grade posted on the inside cover. A. Not even A-minus. Marianne Stoeller wrote a lot of detailed comments on my stories, and at the very end she included a note asking me to see her during office hours, as soon as is convenient.

I rush there the very next day, wondering why she might want to see me.

"Come in, Ellen," she says cheerfully as I enter the office. It's still wonderfully chaotic. I remove a package from the seat before I sit down.

"Oh, that must be the volume of poetry that a former stu-

dent just had published — I've been looking all over for it."
She laughs. "Would you care for some coffee?"

"Sure," I say, and I watch as she goes to a small white coffeemaker and pours some of the dark liquid into an earthenware mug. She hands it to me, and the mug feels reassuringly heavy and warm in my hands.

"I had you come in so we can discuss your stories."

"I can't believe I got an A," I blurt. *Great,* I think. *Now she'll take it back.*

"You deserved it for all your hard work," she says. "In fact, everyone in the class deserved their grades." She says this with a special lilt in her voice.

"Everyone got A's?" I venture.

Marianne Stoeller smiles a bit foxily. "As I said, everyone deserved their grades, and I hope you'll all take it as encouragement to keep writing."

Leave it to this wonderful teacher. I wish all my classes here were like hers.

Marianne Stoeller takes a sip of her coffee. "You've really come a long way since the beginning of class, Ellen," she says. "Of course you have a long way to go, too, but your last set of stories formed the first buds of a charming collection."

Happiness bursts in a flood over my face.

"I call them my Arkin stories," I tell her. "The town in the stories is a lot like Arkin, Minnesota, where I grew up."

"I see," she says. "What are you planning to major in?"

"I'm premed," I say. "Either bio or chem, but I'm not sure which."

"You wouldn't consider something else — literature, perhaps?"

I shake my head. "I've always wanted to be a doctor."

"But the girl in the stories seems to want to be a doctor largely because of the pressure placed on her by her doctor father."

I laugh. "My father *is* a doctor," I say. "And he does put a lot of pressure on me sometimes, but unlike the girl in the story, I truly want to be a doctor. I want to help people. But after taking your class, I want to keep writing, too."

"Good," Marianne Stoeller says. "That's what I want to hear. Would you be willing to meet regularly with me — say, once every two weeks — to do some revisions on your stories?"

"Of course!" I exclaim, almost leaping out of my chair. "I'd be honored."

Marianne Stoeller looks pleased. "How does four o'clock on alternate Wednesdays sound?"

"Great," I say, noting thankfully that I don't have any labs or classes at that time. Revising the stories will probably be time-consuming, but it'll be worth it to work with Marianne Stoeller.

"May I ask you a question?" I say, suddenly emboldened.

"Of course," she says. "Ask me anything you want."

"Why didn't we study any of your stories in class?"

"Good question," she says, leaning back in her chair.

"I really admire your work," I add. "A high school teacher gave me *Stories from Above and Below* as a graduation present, and I've read it several times."

"Really?" She looks pleased. "What stories are your favorites?"

"'Arapaho Dreams,' 'Edith's Day Off,'" I say. "And 'Roseland,' definitely."

"I'm glad you like them," she says. "We don't look at them in class partly because I'm too close to my own work to be a good critic. Also," she continues, "there was an incident in my early career that has left me sort of gun-shy. My first writing job when I was fresh out of graduate school was at a tiny college in South Carolina. It was a lovely place, and I was very lucky to secure such a position, especially having no teaching experience.

"The reason I got this job, I believe, is that I'd already had two stories published in a prestigious literary magazine. I was feeling pretty good about myself — slightly cocky, you might say. In my class I included those two stories in the curriculum as well as an unfinished work, to give the students a feel for the revision process."

Marianne Stoeller sits back; she has the look on her face of someone who has just tasted something very bitter.

"Unfortunately, that work-in-progress had a very fleeting reference to masturbation in it. One of my students showed it to her father, a trustee of the school, and all hell broke loose."

"Over that?" I say with disbelief.

Marianne Stoeller nods. "What it came down to was that I'd have to stop teaching the story or lose my job."

"So what did you do?" I take a sip of my coffee. It is still vigorously hot inside the thick walls of the mug.

"This is most embarrassing to recount to you now, considering my stand on the First Amendment," she says slowly, "but I took the cowardly way out. I stopped teaching the story. In fact, I never even finished the bloody thing."

I try to put myself in her shoes, a young teacher at a small school. "That wasn't cowardly," I say earnestly. "You didn't let it stop you from continuing to write and teach."

"True," she says. "But if I've learned anything from my life, it's that if you're an artist, there will always be people out there trying to silence you, and you have to — you *must* — fight it every step of the way. About a year after that, the college managed to rid itself of me anyway. The story, along with my subsequent antiwar activities, was just too much for one genteel southern school to handle."

I sit there for a moment, soaking everything in.

"It's sad," I remark. "I bet the people who tried to censor you hadn't even read your work."

"You're right," Marianne Stoeller says. "Some people are very set about what they like and don't like, even when they haven't seen the item in question."

"But who cares if they like it?" I say. I am ready to explode. "It's your artistic expression."

Marianne Stoeller smiles beatifically at me. "If only I had had that amount of wisdom when I was your age."

When I leave the tiny, cluttered, magical office, I resolve to let myself write about whatever I want — anything the muse presents me with. I want to be clear and honest and true.

Chapter Twenty-Four

SATURDAY NIGHT, Jae's roommate Charlie is out of town, and Jae and I end up in his room.

Jae has nabbed three A's and one B-plus. I don't know how he does it. I'm relieved to see that some of the healthy color is returning to his cheeks.

"So how are your parents?" I ask him. Sometimes when we're in here, I catch him glancing longingly at their picture. I don't even know if he's aware he's doing it.

"I actually think they're happy to be back in Korea," he says. "My father has gotten some temporary engineering work, and he's been calling a lot of his old college friends to try to find something at one of the *chaebol*, the huge manufacturing companies like Hyundai, Samsung, Goldstar."

"Your father is an engineer?" I say with awe.

"An electrical engineer. Nothing terribly exciting."

"But he ran a grocery here? How did he feel about that?"

Jae shrugs. "You have to do what you have to do to survive. My aunt was a physician in Korea, but she never learned English well enough to pass her boards here. And now the store is so much work, I doubt she ever will practice medicine here."

"That's so sad," I say.

Jae reaches into his fridge, extracts a bottle of lime seltzer, and pours it into two glasses. He has started training seriously for his black belt and won't touch anything even remotely unhealthy.

"They're doing it for their kids, Ellen," he says. "The kids will become the doctors here."

"My father gave up a research career to come to America," I tell Jae. "I sure hope Michelle or I end up in research."

"What about your writing?"

"I'll do that too," I say confidently. "I read somewhere that Perri Klass whizzed through her residency at Harvard Med School, knitting booties for her kid during lectures, writing, and being the best student even in the hardest rotation. Heck, I won't even have a kid to worry about, so what's there to stop me from writing and becoming a doctor?"

"I like your style," Jae says, taking my chin in his hand. I love his eyes, I think for the hundredth time. They're so dark, intense. It's puzzling to me now to recall how much I hated my own eyes when I was growing up. I wanted them to be round and blue, and if there had been some way to alter them, I am sure I would have done it.

"So were you there?" I ask. "During the riots?"

Jae looks down, and a section of his hair falls forward, obscuring his eyes.

"You don't have to talk about it if you don't want to," I say quickly. "I'm just curious."

"I was there," Jae says. His voice seems to come from somewhere else.

"My parents always had a good relationship with the people in the neighborhood," he says. "And we had a black employee, Willie, who worked for us part-time. He was a great guy, and he was going to take over full-time when I went to college. So our store was spared the first day. People in the neighborhood actually protected it. When people would come to loot, I'd hear Willie or someone else tell them, 'Kim's cool; don't do it, brother,' and they'd let us be.

"The next day, though, a different bunch came. They were maniacs; I swear they were high on something. Like fools, my mom and dad stood outside, trying to reason with them — telling them that this was our entire life, our dream. You know what those people did?"

"What?" I say, only half wanting to know.

"They called us monkeys, Ellen, told us to go back to Korea. Then they broke into the store and started grabbing stuff — beer, bottles of soy sauce, Pepto Bismol, for God's sake. They just grabbed whatever they could get their hands on. You can imagine the bedlam — my parents yelling, people smashing things, others running out of the store, slipping on smashed tomatoes. I loved those tomatoes that day. I wish all those people had broken their necks."

I put my hand on Jae's arm. The sinews stand out like cords under my touch.

"And then someone tossed a Molotov cocktail — I saw the Colt .45 jumbo beer bottle — and that was it. The store immediately started to burn, and even then I had to practically drag my parents out of there."

"Oh, God," I say. "Oh, Jae."

"And you know what the worse part was, Ellen? I couldn't do anything to protect my family. I'm sure I could've taken a few of those people out with some kicks —"

"I'm glad you didn't," I say. "The crowd would probably have murdered you!"

"Maybe, maybe not," he says. "But it would've been better than standing around just letting it all happen to us."

"Were you scared?" I ask.

Jae drops his eyes again, shakes his head.

"No," he says. "I was so angry I was crying. And when the store started to burn, in a weird way I became calm — it was all over. I didn't even care what happened anymore. It was all over."

"Your parents didn't have insurance?" I ask.

Jae looks at me as if he can't believe his ears. "Ellen, insurance companies don't give out policies to stores in South Central L.A. My parents were barely making it as it was."

"I'm sorry," I say lamely. "I didn't know."

Jae softens, looks me in the eye.

"Of course you didn't know," he says. "You grew up in Minnesota. Now, why are we talking about all this on a Saturday night? It's our first night together in weeks."

"One last thing," I say. "Is what happened to you in L.A. the reason that you're in the Korean student group?"

"I guess," he says. "I joined KASH because Sookie suggested it. I knew her before I came here."

"So Sookie's from L.A., too?" I ask.

Jae nods. "Her family owns — or I should say owned — a liquor store in South Central, not too far from our store.

I am amazed to know that Sookie is also a survivor of the riots. She and Jae go around so uncomplainingly. I don't see how something that horrible can happen to you and not rule your life.

"Growing up in Minnesota has made me feel so cut off," I say. "I'm a Korean American, but I hardly know what that means." Then a thought occurs. "Do you think I could go with you to your next KASH meeting?" I ask. Joining the group can't make up for decades of ignorance, but it could be a start.

"Of course," he says. "I would've asked you earlier, but I didn't want you to think I was pressuring you or something."

"I love you, Jae-Chun Kim," I say as we meet in an embrace. The celadon pendant presses hard into my flesh.

Chapter Twenty-Five

I PICK "Jessie's Pride" as my first story to go over with Marianne Stoeller.

"I like this one a lot," she says to me. "It's gritty, very honest."

She swivels around in her chair and puts her pen up to her lips. "But I do think that the personalities of your narrator and the Jessie character might be too close to each other. I get the impression that your narrator is an intelligent, sensitive person, while Jessie is, should we say, a bit coarser — the bad language, the dysfunctional family. In your rewrite, you might try to augment the character of the narrator up and the Jessie character down, so to speak, to provide sharper contrast."

I nod. Since this story is so autobiographical, I felt uncomfortable attaching any negative details to the Jessie character, so whenever I did so, I bestowed similar characteristics on the narrator for fairness.

But that's why fiction is fiction. It often consists of embroidering on, exaggerating, revising real life.

"Thanks," I tell my teacher. "I can't wait to begin rewriting."

*

On Saturday, I am writing about Jessie when she calls me.

"I'm not calling about anything in particular," she says. "I just want to blab."

"I just sent you a letter," I tell her.

"Good," she says. "I love getting your letters. But I miss all the spontaneous blabs we used to have."

"How are things?"

"Pretty good. Not much new to report on my dad. Mike's hockey career at UMD is going pretty well. And he's decided to major in business administration."

"Sounds very respectable," I say.

"How's *your* main squeeze?" Jessie asks.

"Not too bad. We've made it to second semester."

"Have you slept together yet?"

"Jessie!"

I can hear her chortling on the other end. "Ellen, we're adults now. We're allowed to do that kind of stuff."

"You're engaged. That's different," I say.

"So are you at least planning to?"

"Not anytime soon," I say. "There's so much to deal with — birth control, safe sex, STDs, not to mention the fact that I don't think I'm emotionally ready. Jae thinks we should wait, too."

"I've never met a guy who wasn't emotionally ready," Jessie remarks.

"Jae's a virgin, too," I tell her.

"No way!" she says. "What's the deal — doesn't he like girls?"

"Jessie," I say, "there are guys who wait, you know."

"I guess," Jessie says. "I've just never met any. How long do you think you'll wait?"

"A year, maybe. If we're still going out next year, I think we can consider it."

"Your self-control is amazing," she says.

"Well, you know how it is — you can't step in the same river twice."

"What's that supposed to mean?"

"I don't know, it sounds good."

Leecia walks into the room just as I am laughing so hard that I'm falling out of my chair.

Chapter Twenty-Six

TRUE TO HIS WORD, Jae takes me to the next Korean American Students of Harvard meeting. It's held in the lounge of Currier House, which, Michelle mentioned once, is snidely referred to as the "Third World house" because a lot of minority students choose to live there. I wonder where Leecia and I will live next year.

Jae and I walk into the lounge. There are some people here already; they all seem to be chatting away in Korean. When they see Jae, they throw him an *anyonghaseo* or a plain old *yo!*

"Ellen, is that you?" I turn to see Sookie. She is standing with a chubby guy whose hair is so curly it looks permed. His cheeks look to be the consistency of bread, soft and puffed up with air.

"This is so cool," she says. "Are you joining KASH? I tried to get your sister to come to a meeting once."

I smile, envisioning what Michelle's reaction might have been. Her thought on what she calls "ethnic pride" groups is that they are irrelevant to a premed.

"I'd like to see what's up," I say. "I hear a lot of good things about it from Jae."

"It's a neat bunch of people," Sookie says. "Ralph and some of the others from tae kwon do are in it."

More people come in. More *anyonghaseos.* So many speak Korean. I used to think nonspeakers like Michelle and me were the norm.

The guy Sookie was with goes to the front of the room and stands on a platform. He says something loudly in Korean. People start assembling around him. He says something else, and the crowd laughs. I throw in a chuckle for good measure.

"Sherman," says Jae, "mind speaking in English for a change?"

Sherman looks annoyed for a second, then he says, "Okay, you nitwits, who was eating too much *kimchi*? You're stinking the place up!"

People laugh again. This time I don't bother.

"Okay," Sherman says. "The first order of business is the Hall of Oriental Studies. As you know, we want to get the name changed to the Hall of Asian Studies. Chul, Sookie, and I met with the dean of students to request this formally. His answer was that tradition dictates that its name must stay the same, especially since some alum, now dead, donated the money with the stipulation that the Hall of Oriental Studies would be named after him."

"Screw tradition," says the guy next to me. "They would have changed the name if it were the Hall of Negro Studies or something."

"We actually brought that argument up, but —" Sookie begins.

"But the administration isn't that keen on becoming educated on the proper use of language when it comes to Asians," Sherman cuts in. "The best he could do, he told us, was bring it up at the next board meeting, which pretty much means he's decided to let the issue die on his desk."

"So we have to figure out what to do to bring attention to this," Sookie says, her voice a little louder. "I'm tired of doing lame demonstrations where no one shows up and the Harvard community doesn't care. We have to learn to be more committed and organized, like, say, the African American Students Alliance."

Leecia's group, I think to myself, a little self-satisfied.

"We need to do something drastic," Sherman agrees.

"How about taking over the dean's office?" someone suggests.

"Nah, the Alliance did something like that last semester."

"How about if we picket the president's house?"

"At three in the morning," adds a voice.

"Hey," says Sherman, starting to grin, "I like that. He'll have to come out in his pajamas. Maybe we can get the media to show up — the police, too."

"Sherman, my parents aren't going to like it if I get arrested for trespassing on the president's property," pipes up someone else.

"The *Harvard* police, stupid," Sherman says. "They won't do anything, but it's good media attention. I don't even think it'd go on your record if we did get in trouble — I'll check on it. The next item is the Park case. Who's not up on that?"

I raise my hand, and to my relief, a few other hands go up too. Jae smiles at me.

"Get with the program, campers," Sherman says, annoyed. "Ok-Ju Park is an elderly Korean woman who owns a laundry with her husband in Somerville. About a month ago, she was parking her car in front of the store to unload some stuff, as she has done daily for the past seven years. A traffic cop came up to her and with no explanation wrote her a ticket. Mrs. Park, who doesn't speak much English, protested. When the officer ignored her, she put her hand on his arm, and at that point the guy threw her against the car and proceeded to arrest her. If that weren't enough, a colleague of this thug-with-a-badge also roughed up and arrested her son, who ran to help his mother. Mr. Park has been frantically trying to navigate the legal system, and we at KASH have been helping him with the bail and other support."

A sympathetic murmur runs through the audience.

"So Ok-Ju Park's trial is coming up, and I hope there'll be an ample supply of us to go to the courthouse and picket against this police state. Hopefully, we can make enough noise to attract the media before this case gets lost in the bowels of the system."

A question is burning inside me, and despite my usual shyness at being new in a group, I raise my hand.

"Yes?" says Sherman, peering down at me.

"Uh, why did the traffic cop give Ok-Ju Park a ticket?"

"Why is that important to you?" Sherman asks suspiciously. A few other people give me unfriendly or annoyed looks. Jae gives my hand a reassuring squeeze.

"I'm just curious." I shrug. Sherman puffs his cheeks in and out a few times.

"If it's so important to you, she was in a no-parking zone," he says finally. Then he turns to the next page of his agenda.

"So she broke the law," I say, louder than I meant to.

"Who are you?" Sherman says.

"Ellen Sung," I say. "And my point is this: what's there to picket? Sure, the officer might have been too rough, but the woman broke the law. Also, why is this something KASH would get involved with? People of all sorts of nationalities get in this kind of trouble."

"Ellen Sung," Sherman says, as if trying to remember my name for a later purpose. "This isn't a parking violation case, this is a police brutality case. Do you think the police would've handled a *white* woman like a chunk of meat? Ok-Ju Park is fifty years old. How would you feel if that happened to your mother?"

"Well, I wouldn't be very happy, but —"

Sherman cuts me off. "Enough said. For those of you who want to support the Parks, and justice for Koreans in general, be at the courthouse at two — here are the maps on how to get there. We'll provide the signs."

After the meeting, Sookie and Ralph and other people from the tae kwon do "in" crowd politely avoid me. The only one to stay by my side is Jae.

"I'm sorry I caused such a scene," I say as we start to walk back to the dorm.

Jae is silent. I'm wildly afraid he's mad at me.

"So I assume you're not going to join," he says.

"I guess I can't see supporting someone for parking in a no-parking zone just because she's Korean," I say.

"It's not the parking that's the issue," Jae says.

"Then what is?"

"Ellen, Koreans — and other immigrants — come to this country believing the myth that if they work hard, they can be just as good as any white American."

"Why do you call that a myth?" I say. "Look, your parents came to the U.S. with so little and here you are at Harvard."

"But that's just it — we're made to think we're equal, but in reality we're treated differently. Koreans have been here long enough that we should have tons of Korean American senators, writers, CEOs, but we don't. We have the highest education levels of any immigrant group, but no one seems to notice that our poverty rates, our family income levels, put us not on the level with whites, but with other oppressed minority groups."

"Jae," I say, "In Arkin, my father, the doctor, was one of the richest people in town. My best friend, Jessie, is really smart, but she could never afford to go someplace like this."

"But that's definitely not the norm for Korean American families," Jae says wearily. "Koreans are second-class citizens in this country."

"I didn't realize you were so militant about this," I say, a little uneasily.

"I have a reason to be. Remember, I grew up in L.A. During the riots I saw with my own eyes how the cops and the National Guard were immediately dispatched in force to Beverly Hills while Koreatown was ignored until two days *after* the place burned down. We paid our taxes, obeyed the law — and what did the government do? They basically handed us over to the looters as sacrificial lambs to protect the white areas."

"Is that why so many of the Koreans defended their stores with guns?" I ask.

"There was no other way," Jae says. "When the police abandoned Koreatown and South Central, the Korean community had to take things into its own hands. A network was set up so storeowners could radio for help, and people risked their lives defending other people's stores."

I wonder if Jae was one of those gun-toting Koreans. But there I go again: one of *those*. When I'm one on one with Jae, everything's so easy. He's another human being, a guy, a friend, maybe a lover. I feel I know him so well, yet this episode at KASH proves that I don't. What effect did it have on him to be one of the Koreans involved in the riot instead of one who watched the carnage via the satellite safety of CNN, far, far away from Koreatown?

"I'm sorry I don't agree with you about all this KASH stuff," I say. "I want to, but I can't."

Jae puts his hand on my back, a touch that is unmistakably loving.

"I don't want you to pretend you agree with me," he says. "That's what I like about you. If we're honest with each other, we'll get through it, okay?"

"Okay," I say, but despite it all, I feel troubled.

Chapter Twenty-Seven

"DO YOU WANT to come to my dance show?" Leecia asks me. "I'll tell you right up front that it'll cost you real money."

"Of course," I say, looking up from my organic chemistry textbook. "I don't care how much it costs."

"Wow, I'll be so psyched to have you in the audience."

"I'll get Jae to go," I say, and I buy two tickets from her for opening night.

That Saturday, Jae and I find ourselves in a small theater on campus. It's so tiny, I don't think it could seat more than thirty people. It looks almost like a rehearsal space.

"What kind of dance group is this?" Jae asks me.

"It's called One in the Heart. That's all I know about it," I say, keeping an eye on the door, waiting for the place to fill up. It never does.

An Asian Indian woman with stylishly short hair comes out to address the ten or so of us in the audience through a spindly microphone.

"I'm Smita Gupta, the choreographer, and I'd like to welcome you to One in the Heart. Our purpose is to provide a means of expression for the minority women's community at Harvard through dance, and to preserve the special culture each person brings to the group."

The choreographer excuses herself, and the curtain opens. A bunch of women clad in a rainbow of brightly colored leotards are standing in a line.

The first heavy beats of Crisis gyrate through the sound system, and the line of women, as if one, begins to move. I spot Leecia near the center, in a turquoise leotard. She looks happy. There is on her face a smile of pure pleasure; it is not the strained, plastered-on smile I used to affect for gymnastics meets.

As the song ends, the women all run to the center of the stage and huddle together tightly, motionless. Then the lights onstage go off.

Next, we are presented with five dancers kneeling onstage. They are attired in rather scanty bra tops and bright Kente cloth skirts. I see Leecia down at the end.

The music is a taped recording of African drums, and the dancers leap to their feet with a bloodcurdling yell. As the beat gets more frenzied, they manage to stay together in perfect rhythm, moving with sure, strong, darting steps.

It is only when this dance has ended that I realize that one of the dancers is a Latina, another Asian. I guess I was always under the impression that blacks had a special penchant for dancing — but why shouldn't an Asian be able to do an African dance well?

We see a few more conventional dance numbers and a funny skit about the problems men and women have communicating. Then there's a soloist. She's black, but her striped costume is Korean.

The haunting sounds of the flute fill the room, and the woman begins her dance in slow, deliberate movements. She keeps her eyes modestly downcast as she performs. The effect is very beautiful, ethereal; very different from the other dances we've seen.

"What did you think?" I whisper to Jae after the woman finishes with what I know as a tae kwon do bow.

"Looked great to me," he says. "I haven't seen traditional Korean dance enough to judge, but this looked quite authentic."

For the last number, the women come out in their bright leotards again. The in-your-face beats of Stopps' "The Power" come blasting through the space.

At the climax of the piece, the dancers gather close in the center and then extend their arms, fingers opening like stars. Their radiating limbs become a human flower, blossoms opening, reaching. Then the lights go out and the curtain comes down.

I am on my feet, clapping like a maniac. Jae joins me. Everyone in the audience is clapping, making the noise of a much larger crowd.

Afterward, we wait for Leecia to get changed so we can all go out. I'm bursting with pride.

"That show was terrific," Jae says. "It's a shame so few people showed up."

I shrug. "It's a Saturday night. People want to party, and why would anyone want to spend time watching a women's dance group, much less a women of color's dance group?"

"You sound just like Leecia," Jae says.

"Thank you."

Leecia comes out with some of her friends from the group, and we all go out for pizza in Harvard Square.

"At last we can eat!" exclaims the woman who did the Korean dance as she eyes the steaming pizza set before us.

"Alissa," Jae asks politely, "where did you learn the Korean dance? It was beautiful."

Alissa smiles, and to my surprise gaily answers him in Korean. Jae then automatically switches. I strain to catch a word or two, but I only end up feeling shut out.

"Alissa's mother is Korean," Jae translates for me. "And Alissa grew up in Korea."

"Really?" I say. I hope I'm not too obvious: I immediately stare at her face, trying to discern any Asian features. She is a beautiful black woman, and the most I can see is a slight almond shape in the corners of her eyes.

"*Hankuksaram?*" Alissa asks me. I know she means "Are you Korean?"

"*Neh*," I say, which means yes, but I can't say anything more, even though she is waiting. I see that in some ways she is more Korean than I am. She can dance Korean and speak Korean, while Jae has to translate for me as if I were a child.

A while later, I notice that Alissa and Jae are still talking. She is smiling, punctuating her statements by touching his arm.

Through a haze of green, I see that Jae looks relaxed but wary. This girl is so beautiful, I almost expect him to be flirting back — at the very least. But he's not. He reaches for my pizza-stained fingers. I wonder, what did I ever do to deserve him?

Chapter Twenty-Eight

"OOH," Leecia says as she comes in, "I am so sick of some black men!"

"Your Alliance meeting?" I ask, handing her a freshly made cup of tea.

Leecia takes a sip of the tea and sighs.

"You got it," she says. "It has just recently dawned on me that from the beginning, every group discussion has been 'the African American man this, the African American man that,' with no regard for African American sisters. It's always the black *man*, as if we need to conquer racism first and then deal with the more trivial stuff like women's issues later. That's bullshit — racism and sexism are part of the same evil. What about us women? But none of the guys in the group listens to our concerns.

"Today a few of us suggested that it might be a neat idea to invite Alice Walker to speak on campus. The guys all thought it was a dumb thing to spend money on — some woman writer. Of course, we women didn't take that too lightly, and a small argument ensued. I swear, some of the guys even mentioned PMS! On days like today I feel my sisters and I should break off and start our own group!"

"If it makes you feel any better," I say, "the Korean American group seems to be just like that. When I went to a meeting, I noticed that Sookie was sort of shoved aside by the guys whenever she tried to make a point."

"Male chauvinism must exist in all cultures," Leecia moans. "How are we people of color supposed to get ahead if we can't even get our act together in our own communities?"

"I have to admit," I say, "I didn't agree with most of the stuff I heard at that KASH meeting."

"Oh, really?" Leecia says with interest.

"Don't take me as disloyal, Leecia," I say.

"You can tell me, Pumpkin. My lips are sealed."

"Well, the first thing they were trying to do was change the Hall of Oriental Studies to the Hall of Asian Studies."

"You don't agree with that?" Leecia asks.

"I don't *not* agree with it," I say. "It seems too trivial to get worked up about, though."

"Well, it depends," Leecia says. "But go on."

"The other thing people were all up in arms to protest about was this lady's being put in jail, even though she did break the law, somehow solely because she's Korean."

"What were the circumstances?"

"She owns a laundry, and when she parked in a no-parking zone to deliver some stuff, she got ticketed. Then she put her hand on the cop's arm to stop him, and he arrested her."

"Hmm. Sounds to me like she broke the law," Leecia

says. "I have a cousin who's a meter maid in New York. She says she gets threatened and slapped around all the time. People go psycho, especially when their cars are towed, so she doesn't take any chances if someone tries to lay a finger on her. Listen, if you do the crime, you do the time."

"I agree," I say. "I guess the lady is older — Sherman, the leader, was saying, 'What if it was your mother?' But it doesn't seem right to have a bunch of people picketing the courthouse — against the police state, in Sherman's words — just because a Korean American has been arrested. I'm sure there are Korean criminals just as there are any other kind."

Leecia rolls her eyes. "Some people are so oversensitive it's silly," she declares. "A few folks in our group are like that; they'll say, 'I got a bad grade because of prejudice' when it turns out they didn't study for the class. But you could say that this extremist behavior *is* caused by racism to some degree. In my soc class we're reading Durkheim, and he talks about how social groups in crisis tend to cast blame on forces outside the group, sort of the way your group is blaming the police for a woman's lawbreaking."

"Maybe," I say. "But I guess I shouldn't keep maligning KASH. Jae and Sookie seem really into it, and I did only go to one meeting."

"You can say anything you want around me," Leecia says. "It won't leave this room."

*

I take "Jessie's Pride" back to Marianne Stoeller, and she reads it while I'm there. Her face is expressionless and as motionless as a statue's. When she looks up, her eyes come to life first. She smiles.

"You've done an excellent rewrite," she says.

She writes something on a memo pad and hands me the page. MARIANNE STOELLER, it says on the top.

"I think *The Kenyon Review* is a good place to send it. They're a very old, established literary magazine, but they're always looking for new talent. You can tell the editor you're a student of mine. Let me know what happens."

"You want me to send this story out?" I squeak. "To living, breathing people?"

"Why not?" she says. "Having a story finished is like having a child grow up — you want to send it out into the world."

"You won't be embarrassed if they reject it?"

"Of course not," she says. "Just send it out. See what happens, okay?"

"Okay," I say.

Back in my room, I start by tapping out a cover letter on my typewriter. While I'm composing the letter, I try to decide whether I should mention Marianne Stoeller's name. I don't want to get any special treatment. But they might at least read it more carefully or faster if I mention her, so I do.

I put the story into the mail, feeling a little bit weird about sending it out. I almost wish I could just put it back safe in its desk drawer. But I guess if I want to write — and publish — I have to let these things go.

*

As it turns out, *The Kenyon Review* does read it fast. I get it back within two weeks — rejected. A form letter, not even addressed to me but to "Dear Writer," arrives.

"Save that rejection," Leecia says. "When you're famous, wave it in their faces."

I smile weakly. I've never been very good with rejection. My first story. And Marianne Stoeller said it was good. *And* I mentioned her in my letter. They read it and rejected it with a form decline. At least on the bottom, someone had taken the time to scrawl "Thank you for thinking of *The Kenyon Review.*" They probably want to keep up the good- will with Marianne Stoeller so that she'll send one of her *truly* talented students to them.

"I really, really like this story," Leecia remarks, peering at the clump of papers that has been returned. "I feel like I totally know these characters. Thanks be to God, I've never had a friend who's lost a parent. This story is so empa- thetic."

"I guess *The Kenyon Review* doesn't feel that way."

"Those people are dummies," Leecia says, and she starts to smooth out the sheets. "Do you know what you should do? You should send this to *Sassy.*"

"*Sassy?*" I say. I stopped reading *Sassy* about five years ago, when I stopped reading stuff like *Seventeen.* Some of my friends from Arkin, like Jessie, still read it faithfully, though.

"Your story is about teenagers," Leecia says. "And that's exactly what they want. C'mon, don't let this great story grow cold here in this suite."

Leecia's enthusiasm is infectious. "Okay!" I practically yell.

The two of us run to Out-of-Town News and buy a copy of *Sassy* to find out the name of the fiction editor and the ad- dress of the magazine's office. New York. Big time. I com- pose a cover letter on Leecia's computer while Leecia pounds out an envelope on my typewriter. We stuff everything into it, seal it, then walk it out to a mailbox.

"Someday, I'll tell everyone that I knew you," Leecia says as we head back to the dorm, the orange neon of Out-of-Town News blazing behind us.

Chapter Twenty-Nine

"MY AUNT AND UNCLE in Boston would like to meet you," Jae says to me as we're walking home from the library.

"Really?"

"They'd like to have us over for dinner. How does next Thursday sound?"

"It sounds great," I say, then I add teasingly, "Does this mean we're getting serious?"

"I've always been serious about you," Jae says, without blinking an eye.

*

For the rest of the week, I think hard about a suitable gift to take. What do you get for people you've never met? In the end I cop out and buy another fruit basket.

That Thursday night I actually put on a skirt. I do try to dress nicely for classes — khakis, sweaters — but I draw the line at a skirt and nylons, especially because I have to spend so much time in the lab.

"You look adorable!" Leecia says, handing me the fruit

basket — the same model I gave her family. "His aunt and uncle are going to love you."

"I hope so," I say. "What if they think I'm a moron because I can't speak Korean?"

"Chill out, girl — you worry too much. Jae is the nicest guy; I'm sure he has the nicest family."

There is a knock on the door, and Jae is here. He has on a sport coat and slacks, and his black hair is freshly washed and gleaming.

"You look really nice, Ellen," he says. Leecia shoots me an isn't-he-the-greatest look.

We take the subway, the "T," into Boston.

"I hope it's okay with you that we're going to be dining *chez* Kim's Happy Fruits and Deli," Jae says as we walk hand in hand. "My cousins can run the store, but my aunt and uncle said they'd feel best if they could hang around to keep an eye on things."

"Of course it's okay," I say.

I keep wondering where the store is. The area is quiet and mostly residential. The only commercial thing we've passed so far is a real estate office.

Up ahead I see a light, an awning. A man is sitting on top of an overturned bucket, trimming the stems of carnations.

"Jae!" the man says happily when he sees us.

Jae bows low. "This is Ellen Sung," he says formally.

I don't know whether to bow or shake his uncle's hand.

"Hello, Ellen." Jae's uncle extends his hand, and I grasp it; it's cold and chapped.

He leads us into the cheerfully lit store. The space is occupied by a salad bar in the middle, dry groceries on one side, flowers and meticulously stacked produce on another, and refrigerator cases full of beer and soda on the third. The fourth side houses the register behind a long counter filled with a wide assortment of things: single-serving packs of vitamins, beef jerky, nail clippers, batteries.

"This is my cousin Gina," Jae says, introducing me to a teenage girl behind the cash register. She is rearranging a display of cigarettes.

"Hi," she says to me.

"I recognize you from Jae's pictures," I say. "You're the one with the funky sunglasses."

"The family ham," Gina agrees.

I wonder where we'll have dinner. There isn't a single chair or table in the place.

Jae's uncle says something to Gina in Korean, and she answers seamlessly. It's amazing to me to hear someone speak "American" one minute and then turn around and launch completely, fluidly into another language.

"We go in back," Jae's uncle says to us.

Jae and I follow him into a small back room. There, a tiny woman who reminds me of Mom greets me with a hug.

"I've heard so much about you, Ellen!" she says, beaming.

We are surrounded in the storeroom by huge bags of rice, stacks of empty soda bottles, pet food. "Sorry it's not so pretty in here," she says.

"It's fine," I say, proffering the fruit basket that Jae has been carrying for me. A little farther down, a couple of cases of apples and oranges wait patiently. The Kims probably need more fruit like a hole in the head.

"What a beautiful basket of fruit," says Mrs. Kim. "Thank you very much."

"Thank you," echoes Jae's uncle.

"*Chunmaneyo*," I say, the Korean for "you're welcome."

Both Mr. and Mrs. Kim smile delightedly, and they both bow from the waist, sort of the way we do in TKD.

Jae puts a hand on my back approvingly.

Farther back in the storeroom is a table neatly set with a cloth and utensils, including chopsticks. A bare bulb sits over it, and the window faces out into the blackness of an alley.

"Not so fancy," says Mr. Kim apologetically.

"Really, this is so nice of you," I say.

Mrs. Kim has made rice in a rice cooker plugged into the wall. Jae and I go out and get food from the salad bar, which has both hot and cold selections.

"The cellophane noodles, *japchae*, are really good," he points out. "So are the *kimbap*, the seaweed rolls."

"Your aunt makes all this food every day?" I say in awe. On the hot side are steamed green beans, macaroni and cheese, some kind of beef dish. The cold side offers all sorts of cut fruit, the seaweed rolls, Chinese-style sesame noodles, chicken salad, tuna salad, cut vegetables of every sort.

"Some they just buy and heat up," he says. "But all the Korean stuff she makes herself." He looks proud. "All the kids help. At Christmas we were making those seaweed rolls like maniacs."

"This all looks so yummy," I say. "But where are the customers?" There was one person in the store when we came in, but he's gone.

"It's busiest during the day and early evening," Jae says.

"Lots of yuppies, overworked mothers, and people who can't be bothered to cook come in. Around dinner, the place is packed and everyone needs to be working. That's why Aunt and Uncle told us to come a bit later."

"When do your cousins get their homework done?" I ask.

"They get it done in the early morning, or when there's a lull in business. They're straight-A students, by the way."

Jae encourages me to load my plate up.

"I don't want to eat up all the profits," I say.

"No, they'll be flattered."

In the back, Jae's aunt and uncle are eating mostly rice and what I recognize as *kimchi*, hot pickled cabbage, with just a little bit of meat on the side.

"The food looks delicious," I say. Both of them smile at me happily.

As we eat, the conversation mostly centers on Jae and me. Mr. and Mrs. Kim ask us how things are at Harvard and where my parents live. I'm dying to ask them what running a grocery is like. From seeing Mr. Kim's hands, I think I know the answer: it's a lot of hard work.

I remark on the prettiness of the seaweed rolls: white rice and colorful pickled vegetables rolled in dark green seaweed.

"It is simple to make — looks nice, yes?" says Mrs. Kim delightedly.

"Very nice," I say. Tasty, too. In fact, everything tastes great: the clear noodles are supple and delicately spiced, the *kimchi* (in small doses) is garlicky and challenging, the seaweed rolls are earthy and refreshingly light. I'm usually not a big fan of salad bars, which I associate with weird concoctions held together by gallons of mayonnaise. But this food tastes wonderful, fresh. Would it taste any better if we were eating in a fancy dining room? I don't think so.

"So how you like Boston?" asks Mrs. Kim. She says it "*Bah*-ston," with a complete Boston accent, like the people in Store 24. Coming from someone who looks so much like Mom, it seems totally incongruous. I try not to giggle.

"I like it fine," I say, a wide grin spilling over on my face.

Mr. Kim, I notice, doesn't speak as much. He listens carefully and nods his head a lot. I get the feeling Mrs. Kim, with her better command of the English language, probably deals with the customers more.

When we're done eating, I'm quite full, but the Kims insist that Jae and I take fresh fruit and whatever else we want home in true salad bar style, in those clear plastic containers. I make sure to take some cold steamed green beans for Leecia, a big bean fan.

"You sure you got enough to eat?" Mrs. Kim asks with concern as we prepare to leave, a bag in each of our hands. I can see Gina behind the cash register; she's reading *Moby Dick*.

"It was so wonderful — *kamsahamnida*," I say.

Jae and I go out into the now frigid Boston night. His aunt and uncle come out without jackets to bid us goodbye.

"Go back in; you'll catch your death of cold," Jae says. I can hear the love in his voice, and something in my throat catches.

We leave them waving in the night and head back to the T, which will take us back to our safe-and-sound fortress, Harvard.

Chapter Thirty

SURPRISINGLY, organic chemistry is easier for me than inorganic chemistry. Everyone talks about how this class is the big "weeder," but I actually find organic molecular bonding kind of interesting. Maybe I'll major in chem now. My choice keeps changing. Leecia is certain she wants to major in Afro-American studies. Jae isn't sure what he wants to do, so he's taking all sorts of classes.

This semester, I'm taking another bio, orgo, physics, and for my elective, an American literature course, which will satisfy one of my core course requirements. In all, a pretty good semester.

"You know," Sookie says to me on a Friday, a Jae-less tae kwon do day, "Jae's black-belt test is coming up."

"I know," I say. "I don't think he has so much as looked at a potato chip since Christmas."

"We should do something for him, since this test is so special."

"How about a surprise party?" I say, suddenly inspired. "Jae is always Mr. Plan-it. Let's do something wild and spontaneous."

"That sounds like a great idea," Sookie says. "But where should we have it? My roommate hates parties."

"We could have it in my suite," I tell her. "My roommate won't mind."

"You sure?" Sookie asks.

"Oh, yes, Leecia will definitely be part of the party," I say.

"Okay, great. I'll get Ralph to go to a Korean food market and pick up all those goodies that Jae-Chun likes. How about if I take care of the drinks and chips?"

"Sounds good. And I'll get the decorations and stuff," I finish. "And maybe a cake."

*

When the day finally comes, I leave Jae alone so he can concentrate. He says he's going to have a light dinner and then sit in his room until it's time for the test. Leecia and I go out to buy food, then get the room ready. We buy a CONGRATULATIONS sign plus individual letters to spell out Jae's name. The clerk can't figure out why we're buying an A, an E, and a J.

"It's someone's name," Leecia says breezily as we leave the card store.

"I swear," she says later. "Leave it to a white person to think everyone's name has to be Tom, Dick or Harry."

Ralph calls us right before dinner to ask if we can stop at the Korean market for him. "I'm so sorry," he says. "I totally forgot, and I have to go to the gym in a few minutes to help Master Han set up."

"No problem, Ralph," I say. "Just tell me how to get to the store and what I should buy."

Leecia and I head out one more time.

The store is near MIT, so we have to take the T to get

there. We wind our way through a weird neighborhood to a small, decrepit-looking store that has Korean lettering (indecipherable to me) under its ORIENTAL FOODS sign.

"Hmm. Another one of these Korean deli things," Leecia muses as we enter the store. A tinkling bell announces our arrival.

This store, however, doesn't look anything like Jae's aunt and uncle's store. This one has no flowers or milk, only dusty shelves piled with mysterious packages, all labeled in Korean. In one corner are pans of water with floating things like bean sprouts, mutant-large carrots, tofu.

The clerk, a grim-faced Korean lady, looks us up and down but doesn't ask if we need help. I glance down at my list. On it I'd written, as best I could decipher over the phone, *dok, kangchong, yakgwah.* In the aisle closest to me are bags of what look like salted, dried minnows. I hope they aren't one of the things on the list.

"I guess I'd better ask," I say to Leecia. I go up to the lady and smile as I approach, but she doesn't smile back.

"*Anyonghaseo,*" I say.

The lady stares at me with the sort of rude fascination you'd give a gory car accident.

"Uh, I'm looking for *dok, kangchong,* and *yakgwah.*"

The lady looks at me again, shakes her head, and snaps, "No understand!"

I repeat myself slowly, enunciating these Korean words that I don't even know. She still shakes her head.

This is going to be harder than I thought. I get out a piece of paper and write, phonetically, the Korean letters for the words.

The woman peruses the paper and shoots me a what-is-this look.

I sigh. "I give up, Leecia," I say. "I think Jae is just going to have to do without."

"Let's try one more time," Leecia says. "The store isn't that big. Did Ralph describe to you what it is we're looking for?"

"Sort of," I say. "The *kangchong* is Jae's favorite. They're made of puffed rice and rice syrup. He said they either look like tiny Rice Krispie bars or huge white Cheetos."

"I'm an expert on Rice Krispie bars," Leecia says determinedly. She disappears down an aisle.

What a difference between this store and the Kims'! I think, somewhat unhappily. What is this lady's problem? Doesn't she want our money?

*

I step halfway out the door to cool off for a moment.

"Hey, are these the ones?" Leecia reappears holding a cellophane bag containing little bricks of puffed rice.

The woman is suddenly right beside us. "Where you go with that?" Her arm shoots out and grabs Leecia's.

"Hey!" says Leecia, trying to pull her arm back.

"You steal — I saw you," the woman says.

Leecia glares at the woman. "I did not steal this," she says. "You weren't helping us, so we're trying to find the stuff ourselves."

"You steal," the woman says again. She is wearing white socks and sandals, an incongruous combination for February.

"My friend did *not* steal," I say loudly. "She was just

· 155 ·

showing me what she'd found. It's my fault for standing over here."

"You're accusing me because I'm black, aren't you?" Leecia says calmly, almost analytically.

"No understand," the woman says.

Certain parts of me are collapsing inward, like a house of cards. I'm embarrassed, angry.

"Let's go, Leecia," I say. I take the bag from her, step back inside, and toss it on a nearby shelf.

"But what about Jae's stuff?" Leecia asks.

"It's a surprise party, remember? He won't notice that anything's missing, and there's no way I'm going to give this lady any of my money."

Leecia walks calmly away, but I have an almost irresistible urge to go back in and tear down one of the shelves, to show this lady what an uncivilized witch she is. I follow Leecia, anger still blistering my skin from below.

"I'm sorry, Leecia," I say as we make our way back to the T.

"You don't have anything to be sorry for," she says gently.

"I feel it's my fault."

"Yeah, the Hindenburg was your fault, too," Leecia says. "You're not responsible for the behavior of every Korean person on this earth."

"Well," I say, "I think she was definitely being racist."

Leecia shrugs. "They come in all colors — strange, but true."

"She shouldn't have treated you that way," I say.

"Don't worry about it, Pumpkin," Leecia says, putting

her arm around me. "We'll still have one hell of a party tonight, even without those little salted fishies."

*

After Leecia and I decorate the room, we head to the MAC's main gymnasium, where the special black-belt test is being held.

A large audience of spectators is occupying the bleachers and the gym railings. On the floor, the other student taking the test is beginning to stretch out. He has a brown belt, which, Jae told me, is the equivalent of a red belt. Ralph, Sookie, and the other black belts are in uniform and waiting on the sidelines. Master Han, formal in a dark suit, is sitting on a fold-out chair in the middle of the floor next to two other Korean gentlemen.

"That's Master Han, our teacher," I point out to Leecia. "The really severe-looking one."

"They all look severe to me," Leecia notes. "What are the other two there for?"

"I think they're judges," I say. "For the lower belt tests, Master Han does all the judging himself."

I finally see Jae enter the floor. He's wearing his Harvard tae kwon do jacket over his white uniform. His face looks intense, unreadable.

Master Han claps his hands and the two line up. They go through the *kemahseh,* shouting enough for an army.

"That is so cool," Leecia whispers to me.

Master Han starts by asking the two some questions about tae kwon do. Jae correctly answers the Korean names of all the various techniques.

"Jae has an obvious advantage over the white boy, don't you think?" Leecia whispers.

The two go through forms together, and as expected, they are very precise.

Then Jae sits down, and the brown belt, with an armful of boards, goes to the front. He bows deeply to the solemn Korean men and motions to a couple of the black belts, who run up to hold the boards for him to break. Sookie goes right up there with the guys.

The student carefully tests the distance between the boards and his foot. At some kind of signal, he blasts through a stack of three boards with a side kick, a two-board stack with a front kick, and another two-board stack with a punch. It all happens in a blur; the boards all divide and clatter to the ground. Everyone applauds and the relieved brown belt takes his broken boards and sits down.

A little Korean boy (Master Han's son? grandson?) runs out with a big janitor's broom to sweep up any remaining splinters.

Now it's Jae's turn. I'm surprised to find that my hands are sweaty.

His boards are so thick that they have to be taped together to form a stack, and all of the available black belts are summoned to help hold them.

What happens next is truly dazzling: Jae starts from a relaxed standing position, jumps up and spins around to kick, at head height, four thick boards. He lands, jumps again, and knocks out three more boards with a flying side kick. For his last technique, he hits three boards with a bareknuckle punch.

There's a crack, but the boards are still intact. A gasp

passes through the audience. Jae's face is impassive. He is staring at the boards, flexing his hurt hand slightly.

"That is sufficient," Master Han says. "You've done well with your flying kicks."

Jae continues to stare.

"I'll try again, sir, " he says. "If I may."

Master Han's eyebrows flutter a little, but he nods.

Then, before any of us have time to blink, Jae sails his fist into the boards with an ear-splitting *kihap*. Six pieces fall to the floor. Everyone cheers. I feel like crying.

"Jae sure is something!" Leecia exclaims, then she whistles out loud, after the place has quieted down. The test is still going on — Master Han still has to hand them their belts — and a few kids around us turn to look at Leecia.

"Yes?" she says to them.

I don't want to embarrass her, so I whisper in her ear, "I think the test is still going on. We're supposed to be quiet."

"Oh, sorry," she whispers back. "I'd think you'd want to be whooping it up right now. This must be an Asian thing I don't understand."

I don't know if it's Asian or not, but it's not her fault — how's she supposed to know?

Master Han ceremoniously hands black belts to the two guys, and everyone claps again. Leecia and I holler.

When I meet Jae after he has showered, his hand is bandaged, like a mummy's.

"Shouldn't you get it x-rayed?" I say worriedly. I sound like a doctor already.

"It's just a flesh wound, ma'am," Jae says, grinning. He must not be in too much pain if he can smile like that.

"I'm so proud of you," I say, steering him around the

gym for a second time. I can't see Leecia or Sookie or Ralph, but I want to make sure everyone has enough time to get to the suite. "I've got a silly gift I've made you back at the room."

"I'm supposed to meet Ralph and those guys for drinks," Jae says apologetically.

"This will only take a minute," I say. "They'll understand."

"Well, okay." Jae shrugs. "But you know how I like to be on time."

"I know." I sigh. "Loosen up a little."

I try to get us to walk back to the dorm as slowly as possible. We enter the suite, and I can't believe everyone is packed in there, hiding.

In the dark, Jae and I bump around for a few seconds. The plan was for someone to hit the lights once we got in, but it's not happening.

"Can't you find the switch?" Jae says, kicking over something.

"Uh, it's not where it usually is," I say inanely. Then the light clicks on.

"Surprise!" everyone yells.

"Oh, my God," says Jae.

Leecia drags out the cake we bought; it has a frosting drawing of a slightly surreal-looking guy doing a tae kwon do kick. BLACK BELT KIM! it says. It took us about a half-hour to tell the lady what we wanted.

Jae throws his arms around me. "So where's my present?"

"Smart aleck," I say.

Sookie breaks out the chips and Leecia starts to cut the cake.

"You are *sooo* amazing, Jae Kim," Leecia says, handing him the first piece. I beam with pride.

We all eat and drink and I introduce Leecia to some of the other people from tae kwon do. She fits in perfectly; I knew she would.

"So where'd the *kangchong* and *yakgwah* go?" asks Ralph, as I knew he would.

I open my mouth to tell him about our misfortune with the rude Korean lady, but Leecia steps forward.

"We got lost," she says, "and couldn't find the store in time. Sorry."

"It *is* in a kind of nondescript building," Ralph says. Then he adds regretfully, "But they have a lot of neat stuff there."

"I'm sure they do," I say, and Leecia and I smile in complicity.

Jae kisses me when everyone else, except Leecia, has gone.

"Thanks, Ellen, you're the best," he says.

"It was Sookie's idea too," I say. He keeps kissing me.

*

At the next tae kwon do class, Jae wears his new black belt. He sneaks me a grin right before we line up, then he goes right up to the first row.

Chapter Thirty-One

I HAD TOTALLY forgotten about KASH, but one day in April, I suddenly see KASH signs plastered all over campus. The notices have a picture of some rap star on them, and underneath they say something about a Professor T and stopping racism at Harvard Spring Weekend.

I don't know much about rap groups, so I inwardly shrug and keep walking. I make a mental note to ask Jae what's going on.

*

"This Professor T thing is really turning into a mess," Sookie says to me as we're stretching out after tae kwon do class.

"Oh really?" I say noncommittally. I still haven't gotten around to asking Jae about it.

"You know who Professor T is, right?"

I shake my head.

"You don't?" she says incredulously.

"No," I admit. "I saw some fliers on campus, but I didn't read them very closely."

"You've seen the news, though, haven't you?"

I shake my head again. "Leecia has a TV, but I don't watch it."

"Professor T is this rap singer who's been invited here for Spring Weekend," Sookie says. "He has this song called 'Get Down, Nuke Koreatown,' which basically says that blacks have been 'dissed' by Korean storeowners for too long and that people should go out and kill Koreans, burn their stores down — those that are left, I suppose."

A cold pit begins to form in my stomach. Sookie shakes her head in disgust. "This anti-Korean racism is new for Professor T, but on that album he has the usual anti-Semitic songs, and the misogynist ones."

"Really?" I say unbelievingly. "What kind of sick group invited him here?"

"The African American Students Alliance," she says.

Leecia's group? That can't be. If Professor T is racist, Leecia wouldn't let him get within a hundred miles of here. Maybe Sookie is misunderstanding something.

"Is Professor T really that bad?" I ask. "I mean, the administration okayed the request, right?"

Sookie sighs heavily. "That's because it's the African American Students Alliance who invited him. The administration knows if it says no, they'll scream racism."

I feel a twinge in my hip as I bend to stretch my right hamstring. "This doesn't make sense," I say. "*You* know my roommate Leecia, what a sensible person she is — she's in the Alliance."

Sookie doesn't appear to have heard me. "I just can't believe that so soon after the L.A. riots, this guy has the audacity to try to cash in on all those bad feelings," she says.

"We haven't even had a chance to rebuild yet, and I bet someone's going to come tear us right back down."

"Were you there, during the riots?" I ask.

"No, I was visiting relatives in Michigan. But my parents were. Even after the store had burned to the ground, looters still went in to steal scrap metal. The excuse they gave my parents — who were standing right there — was that our business was built on money from the neighborhood, so our stuff was really theirs. They never considered that both my parents worked sixteen-hour days, including at really dangerous times, to support us. My dad had an ulcer even before the riots."

I don't know what to say. I can only shake my head.

Sookie rises and straightens out her belt. "Lee Sook-Hee," it says in gold-embroidered Korean letters on the black.

"KASH is definitely going to take some kind of action, and it'd be great if you'd get involved, Ellen," she says before she turns to go to the locker room.

*

"Hey, Leecia," I say, keeping casual, as she comes in that night. "What's the deal with this Professor T thing?"

"Oh that." Leecia sighs as she puts down her bookbag. "As you can probably guess, your friends in that Korean Power society are busting a gut over his coming to campus Spring Weekend."

"Well," I say carefully, "Sookie seemed pretty upset about it."

"Sookie's great," Leecia says. "But I think the group as a whole is overly sensitive. They're making a mountain out of a molehill."

"I don't know anything about this guy, but why didn't

you play it safe and invite someone like M.C. Wrench, or even better, Harvey Harve?" I say, half jokingly. Leecia hates Wrench, and Harvey Harve even more.

She makes a gagging noise. "You know, the thing people who don't like rap don't understand is that it's more than just pop music, Pepsi commercials, and selling underwear. It's an art form, drawing on old African rhythms and story-telling traditions to express the concerns of the African American community."

"But 'Get Down, Nuke Koreatown'?"

"Hyperbole in rap is one of the things that makes it so misunderstood," she says. "And it's not like there isn't vio-lence in white rock 'n' roll — look at the Sonic Booms or the Killers. You don't see people boycotting them. No, people shower them with millions of bucks, limos, and MTV awards."

"True," I say. "But why write a song about Koreans when it's such a sore spot in both communities?"

"That's just the point. Unlike plain old bubble-headed pop music, rap serves a political purpose. It provides a forum for African American voices that the mainstream media refuse to acknowledge. America is supposed to be about free expression, right? Well, we want our point of view heard too. If we can't get it on the ten o'clock news, we'll do it some other way, and rap is just one of those other ways."

Leecia scrutinizes the bookshelf, then takes a swipe at it with her finger, as if checking for dirt. "And I have my own feelings about this black-Korean conflict too," she says. "Remember our trip to the deli for the Head of the Charles, and to the Korean grocery for Jae's party?"

"Yeah." Of course I remember the suspicious eyes on Leecia, the audacity of that woman in actually grabbing her.

"It made me think of that black girl in L.A., Latasha Harlins," Leecia says.

The name doesn't ring a bell with me.

"She was the teenager who got shot in the back by that Korean lady."

"Oh yeah," I say. I remember now: the horrifying TV image of a gun going off, the girl dropping like a bag of stones, as if she'd never been alive. That had happened some time before the riots, but for some reason the news stations kept showing that black-and-white tape next to the images of burning buildings and gun-slinging Koreans as part of the riot footage.

"You know, when we were at the first store, I didn't want to make a big deal out of it because it happens to me all the time — with white and Korean storeowners alike," Leecia says. "But the second time, I really felt that if that woman had owned a gun, I could've been Latasha Harlins number two."

I try to picture what that store would look like on black-and-white film for the evening news. I still think we were pretty far from violence then. But the lady did grab her, and Leecia was strong enough to retaliate. But she didn't.

"Well, she didn't seem too fond of me either," I say.

"But she flat-out *hated* me," Leecia says. "And think of what it would've been like if you weren't there."

I try to think again, but my mind goes fuzzy.

"So regarding 'Get Down, Nuke Koreatown,' rap is one of the few outlets we have to express the rage that comes from all the injustices we have to suffer every day," Leecia says. "And when a rapper says 'kill,' he doesn't necessarily really *mean* kill, just like when you say 'I want to kill that jerk,' you don't literally mean it. But our white critics seem to think we blacks don't have the capacity to distinguish between the literal and the figurative."

Something about Leecia's words makes a small light go off in my head.

"It reminds me of Marianne Stoeller's problem at a small southern college," I say. "Some of the people there didn't understand her work, panicked at the mention of masturbation, and just tried to make her shut up."

"It's censorship, plain and simple," Leecia says, nodding. "And there's no place for *that* on the Harvard campus."

"I agree," I say. Maybe Leecia is right, and KASH is overreacting. I can see Sherman getting all upset about it without ever even listening to the song.

"I think it's great that we have a Korean on our side," Leecia says. "If there were more openminded people like you, we wouldn't have all these problems."

"Yeah," I say, although I'm not exactly on anybody's *side*. I should listen to the lyrics myself before I make any judgment.

*

"Ellen," says the voice on the phone, "this is Sherman Ku. I'm calling to tell you about the emergency KASH meeting we're having to discuss actions to take against the pending appearance of Professor T on Spring Weekend."

"KASH?" I say in puzzlement. "Did Jae tell you to call me?"

"No, I'm merely calling all the Korean Americans in the directory," Sherman says. "You don't have to be in KASH to take part in the protest. In fact, the more people we have, the better."

"I don't think I'm interested."

"You're not *interested?*" he says mockingly. "This isn't a question of being interested. This is a question of Harvard inviting a person who is a known racist against Koreans to campus. You *do* want to fight hate, don't you?"

Of course I want to fight hate, I think to myself, but things aren't that simple. Why, with KASH, is everything always a fight, always against something, so quick to cry racism?

"I want to stress the urgency of this," Sherman says, breathing heavily. " 'Get Down, Nuke Koreatown' is a virtual call to violence against Koreans. If we don't do something about it, who knows what could happen?"

"Did you even listen to the lyrics of that song?" I challenge.

"Of course," Sherman says impatiently. "We spent an entire KASH meeting doing that, and we had a Jewish rights organization send us the transcripts of the lyrics. *You've* listened to the song, haven't you?"

"Uh, no," I say.

"Then I invite you to. I still have all the materials in my room."

I should at least listen to the lyrics, I realize, or I'm being a hypocrite.

"I'll listen," I promise him. "But I'll do it on my own, thanks."

"Ellen, all Korean Americans on campus need to get involved. We can't let what happened to us in L.A. happen again."

"Not all Korean Americans are the same, Sherman." I can't believe I'm actually trying to argue with him. "I feel bad about what happened to Jae, Sookie, and you in L.A., but I grew up in Minnesota. I just don't feel the same. I never even met any blacks until this year, and I've only had good experiences."

"I'm not from L.A.," Sherman says. "I'm from Scarsdale, New York, and my parents are both doctors. My father is a famous cardiologist, actually."

"Wait, what's this about 'what happened to *us* in L.A.'?" I say, confused.

"We are one people, Ellen," he says. "When a Korean's store is burned down, that happens to you and me, too. We Korean Americans need to be cohesive as a group or we are powerless. Mainstream America doesn't give a damn about our problems."

With that, Sherman hangs up on me.

What a blowhard, I think. And how odd that with all of his proletarian "power to the people" talk and his insistence on speaking Korean all the time, his family is probably even more privileged than mine. You could hardly call that being a member of an oppressed minority, right?

*

An envelope comes for me from *Sassy,* and it takes me a second to remember that I sent them my story. I open it to find a letter on purple-spotted stationery, and a few sheets of colored carbon paper inside.

"Dear Ellen Sung," the letter reads. "I greet you with the news that your story, 'Jessie's Pride,' has been selected for our July issue. We wish to purchase one-time North American serial rights for $300, and we may ask for a few tiny editorial changes. If this offer is acceptable, please sign the enclosed contract and keep the hot pink copy for yourself. Once again, we are majorly impressed, and look forward to working with you. Sincerely, Jane Kelly, Fiction Editor."

"Leecia!" I scream.

Leecia looks up from her own mail. "You okay?" she says.

"*Sassy* took my story!" I yell. "We did it!"

Leecia pauses, then cries, "You mean *you* did it!"

We jump up and down all the way up the stairs, then run over to Jae's room to tell him the news. He's so thrilled, he hugs both of us.

"I can't believe it," I say. "I totally can't believe it."

Back in my room, I sit on my bed and look at the ceiling. A national magazine is going to publish a story of mine! I have so many people to tell: Mom and Father, Michelle, Marianne Stoeller, Jessie.

Jessie! I'm going to dedicate the story to her, I decide. If not for her, there would be no story.

I call her, even though it's the middle of the day. She's not home, so I leave a message on the machine she and her father proudly purchased from Target at Christmas.

"*Sassy* magazine!" Mom says when I call her. "I'm so proud of you, Ellen. You used to read that magazine all the time."

"When I was in high school," I say. Okay, so *Sassy* isn't *The New Yorker*. But I'm still happy. And three hundred dollars!

I run over to Marianne Stoeller's office. I know she doesn't have office hours today, so I leave her a note.

That night Jessie calls me back.

"I can't believe it — *Sassy*," Jessie says. "You're going to be famous!"

"You will be, too," I say. "You're sort of in it."

"I am?" Jessie squeals. "Am I a character?"

"You're one of the main characters," I say.

"Oh wow, I can't wait to show everyone. When's it coming out?"

"July."

"I don't know if I can wait that long. Can't you send me a copy of it?"

"They want me to revise it a little first. I'll see what I can do."

"You're going to be famous, Ellen, I can just feel it!"

I study orgo before bed. I got an almost perfect score on my last lab. I can't believe how well things are going — with Jae, with classes, with writing, with Leecia, with Jessie.

I thank God for my blessings, too many to count.

Chapter Thirty-Two

WHEN JAE COMES OVER the next night, I feel an unseen but unmistakable tension between him and Leecia. They don't banter back and forth like they used to. It's odd.

"Want to go out for a walk, Ellen?" Jae asks. I nod.

" 'Bye, Leecia," I say. She seems to be very engrossed in her book.

The night air is chilly, but spring is definitely on its way. Even in the city, you can smell the sweet green shoots and buds sprouting up everywhere.

"Is it just me, or is something not right between you and Leecia?" I ask Jae.

"There's a lot that's not right between me and Leecia."

"Is it this Professor T business?" I say with some surprise. "I haven't heard a peep out of you about it."

"It doesn't mean I'm not involved," he says.

"Talk to me, Jae."

"Ellen, I'd rather keep you out of it. I know how close you and Leecia are."

"I can take it," I say.

"You really want to know?" he asks reluctantly. I nod.

"You're aware of the furor surrounding Professor T's Spring Weekend appearance, right?"

"Only sketchily, from what Sookie and Sherman have told me."

"Well, several reps from KASH, including me, went to the African American Students Alliance to try to talk this thing out. But we were stonewalled, totally rebuffed. And you know who was leading the movement against us?"

"No, who?"

"Leecia."

"Leecia?" I say. "How could that be — especially if you were there?"

"Leecia is convinced that the First Amendment will fall if Professor T isn't allowed to perform on campus."

The First Amendment. Yeah, censorship. There is another side to all this.

"Well, she does have a point. This guy has a right to say what he feels in a song."

"Not a song that will incite people to violence against Koreans."

"But it's a *song*," I say. "Sherman's position is so extreme, it reminds me of mothers who sue heavy metal bands after their kids commit suicide. Give the Alliance, their audience, some credit."

"I wish they'd give *me* some credit," Jae says. "I was there when the riots happened. I saw how the kids actually *danced* after they set fire to our store. Young people idolize these rap stars and the violence their music represents. Rap stars have to take responsibility for this power. And if they don't, we, the Korean, Jewish, and women's groups, will."

I shake my head helplessly.

"Professor T's visit here can't go unchallenged," Jae says more gently. "If L.A. taught us anything, it's that we have to take a stand. The government's not going to protect us; the police certainly aren't going to protect us. About the only stores that survived the riots were the ones that the owners protected with guns. It's sad, but true."

"So what do you plan to do — buy a gun?" I say. "Aren't we talking about two different things here? L.A. was horrible, no doubt about it. But this is a case where a group of Harvard students wants to bring an entertainer to perform for other Harvard students."

"I'm not going to let someone who spouts hate like that onto my campus," he says simply.

"So what do you want me to do?" I say. "Leecia is one of my best friends."

Jae turns to face me. Then he places his hand on the spot where my neck connects with my shoulder.

"I don't want you to do anything, Ellen. I've chosen to get in this fight, and you've chosen to stay out of it."

"This is all so messed up," I say. "Friends shouldn't separate along some color line."

"They shouldn't," Jae says, but for the first time, I hear an echo of bitterness in his voice.

*

"So, Ellen," Leecia says as we're walking to dinner, "want to come to the welcoming rally for Professor T next week? If we play our cards right, we might even get to meet him."

"I don't know," I say. "Jae and Sookie are so upset about

all this that I think I should just steer clear until it all blows over."

"You sure?" Leecia says. "How often do you get to meet a celebrity like that? Also, it'll be fun — we're going to have a huge welcome-fest in the Yard. And remember my friend Kalik, the artist? He's doing the coolest spray-paint banner. We're going to hang it from the top windows of our very own Weld Hall so Professor T will see it when he shows up."

"I think I'd better stay in the library and study until this is all over," I say.

Leecia tucks her arm under mine. "You're always welcome to hang with us," she says. "You could be an honorary homegirl! I think once Sookie and Jae and that obnoxious Sherman guy see how talented Professor T is, they'll cool down and everything will be back to normal."

"I can only hope," I say.

*

The *Sassy* editor calls me. She suggests a few changes to the story, and we work on it over the phone. I feel so professional, talking to my editor.

I ask her if I can include a dedication line.

"So there really is a Jessie?" she asks.

"So to speak," I say. "My friend from home, Jessie, did inspire me to write the story."

"We don't do dedications very often, but I think it's a cool idea for this story," she says.

Next, she tells me, the story will be typeset, and in a couple of weeks she'll send me a galley copy to check.

I can't believe it, still.

*

After the last round of good grades in orgo, I decide that I'll major in chem. This decision is met with cheers of approval from Mom and Father, Michelle — and Irwin.

I can't believe that in the space of less than one academic year, I have learned to write stories, made close friends, and decided my major.

In high school, the days seemed endless — that is, I had a lot of time on my hands *and* each day seemed a lot like the one that preceded it. Now, so much happens in a day. My life is gathering momentum to push me past the threshold, into adulthood: growing up, growing old and all that. I used to hate the thought of not being a kid anymore, but now I feel like it's not going to be too bad.

Chapter Thirty-Three

I FINALLY MAKE my trip to a music store in Harvard Square to check out Professor T's stuff. I'm not a big music fan, so I feel a little disoriented among the rows and rows of CDs: jazz, folk, rock, classical, R & B. I make my way around until I find the rap aisle. Some teenage boys with cocked baseball caps and pants practically falling off their behinds are looking at the CDs. I lurk behind the reggae aisle until they're gone.

I then venture into the rap section. Where would Professor T be? Under P for Professor? T for T? I walk down the aisle until I'm suddenly nose to nose with a huge display.

"Professor T: The City Will Burn — THREE TIMES PLATINUM!" screams the sign. Next to it is a lifesize picture of a guy holding a gun in one hand and making a bizarre gesture with the other. He is standing in front of a cliff, and in the red-sun distance is the curvy silhouette of a woman.

I pick up one of the CDs from the display and read through the names of the songs. "Get Down, Nuke

Koreatown," "Yo, Mama," "Power to the People," "Upside your Head [Bitch]," "Put a Bullet in His Big Blue Head."

Slightly rattled, I put the CD back. Maybe these songs aren't as bad as their titles suggest. But I've lost the desire to spend any of my money on it.

I walk back to the dorm and reluctantly call up Sherman to tell him that I'd like to listen to the song.

"I think you'll find the lyrics most interesting," he says.

I don't reply; I only tell him I'll be coming over.

*

Later that day, my mind smolders, then catches on fire. At first I don't mind listening to the funky, danceable beats, the hypnotic tones of a hypercadenced voice speaking words I cannot quite make out.

Then Sherman hands me the transcript of the lyrics, and the meaning becomes all too clear:

> All these years it's been something that you're missing,
> You think you get away with it when it's us you be dissin',
> But from the doors of your stores,
> Some chinks gonna be hung,
> Or taken care of with a gun.
>
> You call me brother then won't advance me a nickel,
> Yellow motherfuckers to blame for they own pickle,
> You be chillin' when you take my dough,
> Then you put my change down on the floor.
>
> This time, brothers, stand up like we should,
> To kick chop-suey asses out of our 'hood.
> So watch out for that gun we aim at your yellow throat
> When we bust yellow asses all the way back to that boat.

You think dissin' brothers is all fun and games,
Then wave bye-bye to your store — it's all up in flames.

I try to think of Leecia, her words about rap being art, creative expression. Art? In those words, all I can hear is evil, destruction. In my mind now, all I can see is Jae and his mother and father, standing amid a pile of smoking ashes. A store that used to look like his aunt and uncle's cozy one in Boston. An American dream vaporized by hate, stupidity, and a match.

"So what do you think?" Sherman says, a self-satisfied look on his face.

"I'm with you," I say, suddenly sure of exactly which side I am standing on. Jae was right, Sookie was right — even Sherman was right.

"We're trying to figure out a way to stage a protest," Sherman tells me. "We think the most effective way would be to somehow disrupt the welcoming party the Alliance is having for Professor T. That way there'll be tons of people already there to pay attention to us."

Do I have any ideas, he wants to know, about how KASH might drop a banner saying PROFESSOR T IS RACIST while the rally is going on? "We need to do something dramatic to get everyone's attention, but how can we get a banner up with all the Alliance people around?"

I think for a minute. A banner . . .

"I do have an idea," I say, feeling only fleetingly like Benedict Arnold.

*

"Hey, Leecia, it looks like rain," I say, peering into the darkening sky as we return to our suite from dinner. "You didn't just store that Professor T banner out on the roof or anything, did you?"

"Oh, no," Leecia says. "There's an abandoned broom closet on the top floor that's perfect for storage. Pretty clever, eh?"

"Pretty clever," I say, feeling vaguely as if I'm in a spy movie. Leecia is not going to be happy with what I'm about to do, but I think ultimately she'll at least try to understand.

*

The first typeset copy of my story arrives for me to check over. It looks so professional in real type. I immediately make duplicates and send them out to Marianne Stoeller and Jessie.

Chapter Thirty-Four

"A RE YOU SURE you want to do this?" Jae asks, stroking my hair as we lie on his bed.

"I'm very sure," I say, staring at the ceiling.

"I won't think less of you if you don't," he says.

"*I'll* think less of me if I don't."

Jae pulls me close. I feel my body soften like wax against the heat of his.

"But what about Leecia?"

"She's a strong person; we're good friends. I think she'll understand why I need to do this."

"Why do you?"

"Jae, when I heard that song, all I could think of was your family, standing by the burned-out rubble of your store."

"But your case is special, Ellen. Maybe you should just let this whole conflict pass you by, to preserve the harmony of your suite, your friendship with Leecia."

"But don't you see, Jae?" I say. "If everyone did that, we'd get nowhere."

Jae combs my hair with his fingers. "I don't know. You'd

think I'd be happier about someone converting to a KASH cause."

"I'm not *joining* KASH," I tell him drowsily. "I'm just taking part in this protest."

"Agreed, then," he says.

*

Sookie has attended countless Alliance rallies to figure out how KASH could do better. She knows the work of the spray-paint artist Kalik well enough to spray an imitation banner with the same violent orange-black-green, graffiti-inspired background. Hers, though, will have a different message: PROFESSOR T IS RACIST.

The night before the rally, KASH convenes again. I had already sneaked Sookie into the Weld broom closet so she could get an advance look at the banner and check out its size. Our banner had to be the same size so the people unrolling it wouldn't become suspicious.

"The banner switch has been done successfully," Sherman says. "And let me mention that our friend Ellen Sung was instrumental in the planning."

Everyone cheers.

"Here is the banner that would've gone up," Sherman says, pointing to two of his assistants. They pin the large sheet to the wall.

The colored background is very much like Sookie's imitation, but the main part of the sign is a picture of Malcolm X holding a huge gun, side-by-side with Professor T. On the bottom it says BY ANY MEANS NECESSARY. It had been easy for me to make the switch: I just waited until the night Leecia had her Alliance meeting.

Now we set about the task of making the signs that we'll

be holding once we make our presence known. When the paint, posterboard, sticks, and hammers come out, the atmosphere is jovial, excited, and we are like kids doing a sixth-grade art project.

I merely put a quote on mine: "Wave bye-bye to your store / It's all up in flames." Sookie smiles over at me as she staples the signs to wooden sticks. I smile back.

Ralph comes over to Jae and me. He pretends to jump-kick me in the head and give Jae an elbow-smash. "Hey, good work, Comrade Ellen," he says to me before moving on to tease Sookie.

Sherman claps his hands. All action stops.

"We're all gathered here in the name of Korean American solidarity," he says, as if he's delivering a sermon. "What's at work here is *jung*, that spiritual bond that keeps us all linked together by blood. Remember, we can't sit here, complacent in our little Ivy League towers, and pretend that we're white, that racist violence can't happen to us. We don't have equal protection under the law, as we saw evidenced so starkly in the Los Angeles riots. We have to stand up and fight for our right to be here in America, fight for our parents' American dreams."

I guess as a joke, someone is waving around a sign that says PROFESSOR T MUST DIE.

"Our goal is to attract national attention, and then to start a nationwide boycott of Professor T and his record company."

That's what Sherman thinks we're all doing this for? A boycott of records? Even if such a thing is successful, who's to say that three more rappers won't rise up in his place?

Aren't we trying to stomp out the hate, to promote dialogue? Admittedly, I'm here largely because of Jae and Sookie. I care about what happened to their families. If not for them, I'd probably still be thinking of the Koreans in L.A. as gun-toting gangsters. Maybe if Professor T knew someone like Jae or Sookie, he wouldn't think of writing these songs at all. So shouldn't we be trying to stake out a middle ground between blacks and Koreans — and other people of color?

Sherman instructs us that tomorrow we should try to hang around the perimeter of the welcoming crowd unobtrusively.

"Act like you're going to the library if you have to," he says. "Then, when the banner's unfurled, that's your cue to come out with the signs. If something goes wrong with the banner plan, I'll yell 'KASH' from the steps of Widener, and that'll be the signal."

He also tells us that if by any chance the Harvard police come around, we should resist arrest by sitting down. "No violence," he says excitedly, "but resist passively."

Jae comes back with me to my room. Leecia has left a note saying she is staying the night at Monica's to watch "Boyz 'n the Hood."

As we bed down in the familiar room, I see that the goofy, lacy card Leecia gave me for Valentine's Day is still tacked on my bulletin board. For the first time, I start to feel serious dread — about what I've done, about how Leecia will feel.

"I wish this were over already," I say to Jae. "This waiting is driving me crazy."

"Yeah," Jae agrees, his knees touching the back of mine. "It's like the calm before the storm."

Chapter Thirty-Five

I FEEL SICK to my stomach as soon as I get up.

"Ellen," Jae says, "there's still time. You don't have to go."

I take a deep breath. This day is going forward like any other. Classes, meals, hanging out. I could make it a normal day if I wanted to.

"Of course I have to go," I say firmly. "I have to see this through."

"Okay, soldier," Jae says, giving me a two-finger salute. "I'll meet you at my room at two."

*

"You sure you don't want to come to the rally with us, Pumpkin?" Leecia asks me as we head out for our morning classes. "Monica is even missing one of her *science* classes to be there."

"I think I'll skip it, Leecia." My voice comes out clear, annoyingly everyday.

"Well, don't blame me for missing the chance of a life-time," Leecia says good-naturedly as she heads to her lecture hall and I break off toward the Science Center.

At two I meet Jae. He has our signs cleverly hidden in an artist's portfolio he borrowed from a friend. The portfolio is like a huge, flat suitcase; it's made out of black vinyl and has zippers on three sides, as if it were created to carry demonstration signs.

We start walking over to the rally site. A sizable number of students are milling around, but not quite as many as I would've expected. On the sides, though, is a full entourage of media: people from the *Globe*, cameras with the logos of local TV stations.

I see Sherman sitting on the steps of Widener, studiously reading a textbook. Under his jacket next to him, the stick from his sign protrudes slightly.

"Everyone's here except for Professor T," Jae observes. I don't see Leecia, but I do spot some friends of hers from the Alliance.

Jae and I stand around talking as if we've just chanced to run into each other. I keep an eye on the top windows of Weld.

Twenty minutes later, Professor T still hasn't shown up. A few people leave, a few more arrive, conserving the critical mass of the crowd.

Finally I see action. Three people, one in each of three consecutive windows at the top of Weld, hold the rolled-up banner like a log between them. I hold my breath as it unfurls to a rising cheer.

PROFESSOR T IS RACIST.

The cheer transmogrifies into a buzz, then an angry cry, as people point at the top floor of Weld.

The banner holders lean out the window and try to read

the words upside-down. Then each of them tries to yank his piece of the sheet inside, with the effect that the banner is only pulled taut across the three windows.

"Let it go, idiots!" yells a voice from the ground. The banner remains suspended a minute more, then gently undulates toward the ground, saying one more time, PROFESSOR T IS RACIST.

By now, Jae has gotten our signs out, and we start moving with the other KASH people to the steps of Widener. Sherman is standing at the very top of the stairs with a bullhorn, trying to start a chant of "Hey hey, ho ho, racism on campus has got to go."

Sookie, Jae, and I stand together, chanting and holding our signs. Passers-by actually stop and pay attention to our demonstration. For a minute I feel an enormous rush of solidarity with the assembled Koreans — even with Sherman. We're united, fighting for something we believe in.

The people from the Alliance, however, soon figure out what has happened and start toward us.

"I don't know what you're trying to prove, but you've disrupted a sanctioned Harvard event," one guy yells, shaking his fist at Sherman.

"Harvard is wrong," Sherman bellows back with battery-powered force. "With a song like 'Get Down, Nuke Koreatown,' Professor T should *never* be allowed on campus!"

"Get out of our faces!" yells another voice, and clenched fists start to rise in the air as the Alliance begins a counterchant of "Professor T!"

"Hey hey, ho ho, racism on campus has got to go!"

The Alliance people start to mount the steps. No one is going in or out of Widener. More people walking by pause, then attach themselves to the crowd like coral.

The Alliance crowd continues to surge forward like a single being. I am pushed out of the way as someone jumps up and tries to take the bullhorn away from Sherman.

I can hear the clatter of running feet now, shouting — and I've somehow lost Jae. There is a firm grip on my arm, and I half expect to see the campus police.

But it's Leecia.

"Ellen, what are you doing here?" Her eyes are glued to my sign.

"I . . . I . . ." Why, why hadn't I thought about what I'd say to her? This was bound to happen. I try to think as we continue to be jostled. Finally, we are spit out at the side of the crowd.

"Ellen, how the hell did the banner get replaced?" Leecia's eyes are full of cold, controlled fury.

This is Leecia, I keep telling myself. *My friend.*

"I won't lie to you, Leecia," I say. "I switched it."

Leecia looks at me in disbelief. "Ellen — you didn't," she says, beginning to shake her head. "Is that possible? You betrayed me, lied to me, stole an artist's work —"

"Don't think of it like that," I plead. "When I finally heard the song — and after knowing what Jae and Sookie have been through — I felt I had to join the protest."

"With the group that you yourself said was wack?"

"I'm not with KASH," I say. "I'm protesting Professor T. His song about Koreans isn't right."

Leecia folds her arms. She looks remarkably composed amid the surrounding chaos.

"What *is* it that you guys are so afraid of?" she says. "The truth? Professor T didn't simply fabricate his song. It's a known truth that Koreans — maybe not you personally — have been taking advantage of blacks for too long. Koreans start their stores in poor black neighborhoods, get rich off black money, and then turn around and snub the hell out of the people — not putting the change in their hands, being rude, accusing them of stealing. The African people can only take so much."

I am struck dumb. I had no idea that Leecia's views about Koreans ran this deep.

"This is crazy!" My voice comes out strangled. "We're talking about Jae, about Sookie."

"Don't forget that Sookie's parents owned a liquor store," she says. "Ever been to the L.A. ghetto, Ellen? There's a liquor and gun store on every block, and the Koreans own them all. If they don't get you with the high prices for food, they get you with the booze, the guns."

"Nobody forces anyone to buy anything," I say, my voice rising a few octaves. "And what is your wonderful Professor T doing for his *people*? He's no social worker — he just gets rich off these racist songs!"

"You don't understand, do you, Ellen?" Leecia says calmly. Her calmness infuriates me. "If you listen to the song, it's clear: the white system breaks our people down, then the Koreans make blood money off them — off gun stores, off baby formula, you name it. It's sick."

"How can you say that? They're just storekeepers trying to make an honest living!" My voice reaches higher, higher. I vaguely notice a bright light, like an interrogator's, in my eyes. Leecia's placidity is driving me wild. How can she be

so coldly analytical about all this? How can she know of
Jae's situation — his heartbreak, his poverty — and still
think the way she does?

"How can you talk about the ghetto as if you understand
it?" I yell. "You grew up in a ritzy suburb, went to a fancy
boarding school, for God's sake. You never had to watch
some stupid creeps burn down your American dream."

Leecia's eyes widen, almost imperceptibly. I know what
I could say to really hurt her — and, God help me, I say it:
"You're not protecting free speech, you're protecting
Professor T's right to sling cheap hate, and that makes *you*
just as much a racist!"

Leecia's jaw clenches. "Racist?" she says in disbelief.

Why did you do this? says a voice inside me.

But I also feel a terrible taste rise up in my throat. I'm past
the point of no return.

"Ellen! Ellen!" Jae drags me away.

Leecia shakes her fist at me. "I can't believe I ever
thought of you as a friend!" she screams — the first time
she has ever raised her voice to me. "You are nothing but a
liar!"

I begin to cry.

Chapter Thirty-Six

B Y THE TIME Jae and I return to my room, I am numb. The light on the answering machine is flashing. I automatically press the play button. Maybe it's someone calling to tell me that this has all been a bad dream.

"This message is for Ellen." It's Jessie. "I just read the story you sent me. I can't believe you did it. I can't believe you ripped my life open, exposed me like some monkey in a zoo, only so you could get your name in *Sassy*. Pathetic. Better save this message because you're never, ever going to hear my voice again."

I tell Jae I need to be alone.

*

At ten, Leecia still hasn't returned home. When the phone rings, I jump on it.

"Ellen?" says Michelle. "Are you okay?"

"No," I say, my voice thick. "Did you hear about the protest?"

"Hear about it?" Michelle says. "Ellen, it was on the local news."

The lights, I suddenly remember. The bright lights.

"They had a shot of you and Leecia arguing, pretty heatedly. What happened?"

"I can't talk about it right now, Michelle." My voice tightens into a dam against impending tears.

"Do you want me to come over?"

I think for a minute.

"Yes," I say gratefully. "Please."

As soon as I hang up, the phone rings again.

"Myong-Ok, Myong-Ok!" My mother's voice. "Are you all right?"

"Of course," I say, hastily composing myself. "Why wouldn't I be?"

"We saw on the evening news," she says. "Some disturbance at Harvard."

The national news! What *more* could go wrong?

"You were fighting some black girl," Father adds, on another extension. "You aren't hurt, are you?"

I can't believe this is happening.

"We weren't physically fighting," I tell them. "That was my roommate, Leecia. She'd never hurt me."

"Your roommate?" Mom and Father say at the same time.

"We disagreed about something happening on campus." I sigh. "It's not what it looked like — we're very close."

"You aren't in trouble with any of the campus authorities, are you?" asks Father.

I sigh again.

"Not that I know of."

That seems to satisfy Mom and Father, at least for now.

Michelle arrives, a worried look on her face. "So what happened?" she says, sitting down next to me. "I almost fell out of my seat when I saw you on TV. You were at some African American Students Alliance demonstration?"

I open my mouth, but only small pathetic noises come out. Then the dam breaks, and a sea of sadness and remorse washes over me.

"Oh, Ellen," I hear Michelle say. There is something remarkably soft in her voice. Her arms fold protectively around me.

"I'm here," she says. "It's okay to cry."

*

Michelle helps me wash my face; she brings me some soup and tucks me in. She even takes my chem problem set to check over.

"I hope Leecia is okay," I say. "It's not like her not to come home."

"Leecia can take care of herself," Michelle says, retiring to the living room, where she has made a bed on the couch.

The next morning, Leecia still isn't back.

"Shouldn't I go to the police or something?" I ask Michelle.

"I think you should check with Leecia's other friends first," she says.

After calling around and leaving messages on answering machines, I eventually make it to physics. Our teacher reminds us that we have a test coming up, and I wonder how I'm going to collect myself enough to study for it. On the way back to the dorm, I run into Sherman. I try to duck my head as he approaches, but it's too late.

"Ellen!"

"Oh, hi, Sherman."

"Things went pretty well yesterday, eh?" he says. "We garnered campuswide attention, got on *national* TV, and made Professor T go back to L.A."

"We drove him off campus?" I say, dully hopeful.

"Well, he had problems with his limo coming from the airport," Sherman says. "But I'm sure when he heard about the campus disturbance, he decided to cancel the whole thing. These big entertainers are always like that — they can't handle a spot of controversy."

I manage to summon up the energy to shrug.

"I think I misjudged you, Ellen," he says. "You seemed sort of naive at that first KASH meeting, but you proved me wrong. What an excellent scene of you and that arrogant Alliance person arguing. Did you see it on the news? It puts to rest the stereotype that Asians are passive."

" 'Bye, Sherman," I say.

Sherman looks slightly surprised. "I'll see you at the next KASH meeting, right?"

I begin to walk away. He doesn't follow.

As I make it back to Weld, I come to a conclusion: if I had known what I know now, namely, that taking part in the demonstration would result in my saying such stupid, hurtful things to Leecia, I would've heeded Jae's advice and gone in spirit only, preserving the peace at home.

But I didn't do that. Instead, I said things I can't take back. And where has this action gotten me, or Jae, or the world at large? I doubt it was our demonstration any more than the car trouble that kept Professor T off our campus. And he undoubtedly went back to his swanky home and will simply cut more records. The rupturing of a deep and loving friendship won't mean a thing to him.

If I could, I'd turn the clock back and do things differently. And I don't usually think that way.

When I reach for the doorknob to the suite, the door swings open by itself. Leecia is in the doorway, on her way out.

We freeze and stare at each other, as if we're on opposite sides of a chasm.

"Oh God, you're back," I say, relief pouring out of me. I begin to move toward her.

"Get out of my way!" she says, walking past me.

"Leecia!" I say, grasping her elbow. She wheels around, shaking my hand off, but she pauses.

"What is it with you?" she says.

"Leecia, I'm so sorry about yesterday, about what I said. I hope you know I didn't mean it. I would never want to hurt you — you're my friend."

"I can't be friends with someone who betrays me," Leecia says. "Or calls me a racist. After my family welcomes you into our home, they have to watch you on TV calling *me* a racist. And who are you to say I don't know anything about the ghetto? I'll always be a nigger to white folks and Koreans — and you know that just as much as I do. You were there when some of those things happened to me!"

"Leecia, I didn't mean what I said. Please believe me."

"I'm way past believing anything you have to say,"

Leecia responds, her chin pointed up, like a weapon. She continues past me quickly.

I turn and walk into the room. Next to the answering machine is a note that Jae called. Leecia hates my guts, yet she's well-mannered enough to give me my messages.

Please, please, please let this be a sign of hope, I pray.

Chapter Thirty-Seven

SEEING LEECIA makes me realize that I have to act fast, and I immediately call *Sassy*. Perhaps there's a chance Jessie will forgive me if I don't publish the story.

Someone at the switchboard answers, then puts me through.

"Hey, Ellen," Jane Kelly says to me. "What can I do for you?"

I get right down to the point. "I'd like you to pull my story, 'Jessie's Pride.' "

"Am I hearing you right?" she says.

"Yes. I'm sorry for the inconvenience."

There is a moment of silence between us. In the distance, I can hear phantom echoes of another conversation going on; two women are screeching with laughter.

"Ellen," she says, "we purchased the rights, and it's an excellent story. What's the deal?"

"It's personal," is all I can say. "I can return the money."

"It's not the money," Jane Kelly replies, suddenly snappish. "It's just astoundingly inconsiderate of you to pull the story after we here at the magazine have put so much work into it."

"I'm sorry," I whisper.

More silence. Then Jane Kelly sighs a deep and mournful sigh. "You're sure you want to do this?"

"Yes."

"You're making a big mess for us," she says. "You obviously don't know much about magazine production."

"No," I say. "I don't."

"I'll see what I can do — it might be too late," she says. "Call me back next Monday."

"I will. I'm very sorry."

Jane Kelly hangs up without any further words.

I call Jessie, but she's not home. I know her father might hear the message, so I say, like normal, "Hi, Jessie! It's Ellen. Call me."

*

Leecia comes back to our suite that night, but she doesn't look at me or talk to me — not one word, not one glance. She merely retreats to the bedroom and shuts the door.

I spend the hours before bed sitting by myself in the common room. I resist the urge to go out, to see Jae, to see Michelle. I *will* stick this out.

The next morning I wake feeling a little more optimistic, but Leecia goes to breakfast early, by herself.

I run into Monica later that day.

"What should I do about Leecia?" I blurt. "She won't talk to me or anything."

"I can see why she won't," Monica says, her eyes narrowing. "What you did to her is something she can't just laugh off."

I throw my hands up in exasperation. "Look, it wasn't a very nice thing I did, switching the banner. The things I said to Leecia were even worse. It was wrong; I was wrong. I apologized. But I never, ever meant it with any kind of bad spirit. Can't you guys cut me a little slack?"

"The banner thing is your business," Monica says. "But what you said to Leecia — said on TV — is everyone's business. I think it's not that you didn't mean it, it's that you don't want others to *know* that you meant it."

"I don't think Leecia is a racist, if that's what you're implying," I say.

Monica smiles sardonically. "Then why did you say it?" she says, turning her back to me and walking away.

*

Jae stops by when Leecia and I are both at home, suffocating in a place that used to seem too big when the other was gone. He doesn't even say hello to Leecia. Leecia ignores him.

"They're showing *When Tae Kwon Do Strikes* in Ralph's room at eight. Want to go?" Jae asks.

"Yes," I say. "I do."

We walk out.

"It's not fair, the way she's treating you," Jae says, anger rasping his voice.

I shrug. "I said and did some pretty bad things."

"But so did *she*," Jae fires back. "She said a lot of hurtful and untrue things, and I'll bet she hasn't said *she's* sorry!"

I shrug again. "Does it matter? What does it mean for the future of race relations when two close friends can't get along?"

The Serbs and the Bosnians, I think. The Jews and the

Palestinians, the Koreans and the Japanese, the Iraqis and the Iranians, the Hindus and the Muslims, blacks and whites, Catholics and Protestants, blacks and Koreans. Where does it end?

"She'll get over it," Jae says. "I think she just feels some kind of need to punish you, which is ridiculous and mean."

Chapter Thirty-Eight

I SOMEHOW MANAGE to get my schoolwork done, even though when I'm not worrying about Leecia, I'm worrying about Jessie. Leecia I see every day, and the coldness in her face is clear evidence that the rift in our friendship has not yet started to heal.

Jessie I neither see nor hear, yet I take it as significant that she hasn't called.

"Why is it that the strongest-seeming friendships can blow apart so easily, as if they were cobwebs, so you're hardly even sure they were ever there?"

I have found my way to Marianne Stoeller's office, and she is listening to me intently as I salt my coffee with an occasional tear.

"After all the good times Jessie and I shared, the times we stuck up for each other, how can she just shut me out of her life? I've called her again and again, and her father says she's not home, when I bet she is. I do one stupid thing and poof! All those years go up in smoke. And on the same day I bombed my friendship with Leecia. I'd never experienced such anger from either of them."

"Ellen, it's often hard to know, and sometimes surprising to find out, what makes the people close to us angry. But I think you're being too hard on yourself. What you did wasn't stupid in either case. Your problem with Jessie — that sort of situation has happened at one time or another to *all* the writers I know."

"Really?" I say. "Even you?"

Marianne Stoeller smiles — a little wanly — and nods.

"Do you remember that character Brett in 'Roseland'?" she asks.

"I just reread 'Roseland' the other day," I say eagerly.

Marianne Stoeller nods appreciatively.

"I had a long-time lover, Jason, whom I thought was going to be the love of my life. He was something like the passionate Brett in 'Roseland.' Well, Jason felt I was giving away intimate secrets about him, about us, to the world."

"Were you?"

"I didn't feel I was," she says. "But he thought so, quite certainly. So to him, I suppose I must have been."

"What happened?"

"After he read the story, that was it," she says, pensively stroking the thick silver ring on her right hand. "He left. He never gave me a chance to explain."

"He stopped loving you because of the *story*?" I say, wincing.

Marianne Stoeller gazes out her small weather-streaked window into the distance. "I daresay he never stopped loving me. But he did leave me, and it was because of the story."

"If writing wreaks so much havoc on your life," I say, "why would anyone want to do it?"

"For a writer, stories are inevitable, Ellen. Think of it this way: everything that's happened in your life has led you to this very moment—to the two of us talking about writing. For me, if I hadn't been with Jason, there probably wouldn't have been a 'Roseland.' "

"What do you think I should do about 'Jessie's Pride'?"

"You really like 'Roseland,' right?"

I nod.

"So you see that even though I caused Jason a lot of pain, and Lord knows he caused me a lot of pain, there was 'Roseland,' and you read it and took my class, and here we are."

"That story was the one that really inspired me to try writing," I admit.

"Then don't throw 'Jessie's Pride' away," she says. "Being published means you have a voice, and some other person might be similarly inspired."

"But Jessie is my best friend," I say. "When it comes down to it, aren't friendships more important?"

"Friendships are one of the most important things in life," Marianne Stoeller says. "But as you know by now, you can't control people. Killing the story is no guarantee that Jessie will come back to you, but it is a guarantee that your story will never get a chance to touch someone. For what it's worth, you might try cutting Jessie's name out of it, and doing the same for all similarly inspired characters in the future."

I leave Marianne Stoeller's office, and I return to the suite to call Jane Kelly. I tell her to keep the story, but to excise the dedication and change the character's name to Jenny.

"You're a pain in the butt, Ellen Sung." I can almost see her shaking her head. "But we're glad to have you back."

"Thank you," I say, although it comes out as barely a whisper.

Chapter Thirty-Nine

TRANSCRIBING PHONE MESSAGES for each other is a form of communication, however meager, that continues between Leecia and me. One day I come in to hear a message for her: "Leecia Thomas, this is the Housing Department. We looked into your request for a room switch, but we're sorry, it's too late in the year for that. Good luck with the lottery for next year."

Leecia isn't waiting out the storm. She is trying to leave. I write this message down word for word.

Okay, I think, *I've done all I can. She can have it her way from now on.*

"Here's your message," I say, handing the piece of paper to her as she walks in the door. She takes it reluctantly, as if she were being subpoenaed, and eyes me suspiciously.

"I'm sorry you can't get out of here," I go on. "But I thought I'd make things as congenial as possible."

I hold up a roll of masking tape.

"Right down the middle," I say. I place the tape, starting up the wall a ways and unrolling it down the room, bisecting the couch, moving over the floor and up the other side.

"You're crazy," Leecia says. These are the first words she's said to me since our exchange in the hall.

I merely smile and do the same thing to the bedroom, marking the boundary between the beds.

"If we can't meet halfway," I say, "we might as well stay on our own sides. You're the one who's wanted boundaries. Up until now, it's all been mental. Let's clear the air and make it physical."

Leecia steers herself around me and dumps her stuff onto her bed.

"Watch it — you're stepping onto my side," I say. She glares at me.

I smile at her, feeling as if something has been accomplished.

Chapter Forty

Dear Jessie,

I'm sorry that my story "Jessie's Pride" hurt you so much. I didn't mean it to. Hurting you is the *last* thing in the world that I'd want to do. I truly only meant it in the spirit of friendship and love. I hope you can find it in your heart to forgive me, but if you can't, I'll understand. As I said before, the story will still run in the July issue, but I've changed the name.

I guess it was dumb of me to use your name, because you and the Jessie character in the story are not one and the same. This was a piece of fiction, not nonfiction, that I wrote. Again, I'm sorry for all the pain that it has caused.

I hope to hear from you.

Ellen

P.S. This is going to be my last letter.

I'm in the suite's living room, writing this. Alone. The

masking tape down the middle has begun to crack with wear.

Leecia still isn't talking. I say hi to her, make small talk. Sometimes I hum to fill in the empty spaces between us.

It must take so much *effort* for her to be like this. Why won't she just get tired of being so proud, so stubborn?

*

The housing lottery comes and goes. From Leecia's phone conversations, I have gathered that she, Monica, and a few friends from the Alliance are going in together. Jae is staying with his current roommate, Charlie. I've recently become friendly with a girl named Stacy who's in my bio study group. I asked her if she'd be interested in going into the housing lottery with me, and surprisingly, she said yes.

Leecia's group gets into its second choice, Currier House. Jae and Charlie get into their first choice — Currier House. Stacy and I and a friend of hers end up in Kirkland, a house by the Charles River, which is what we wanted.

*

Irwin has taken it upon himself to arrange a post–spring break formal for Weld. He promises us live music, lavish decorations, and dancing through the night.

Jae and I, of course, are planning to go. We take a trip to a used-clothing store, Keezer's, and find him a not-too-used tux. For me, Mom goes out to Dayton's and buys a black dress, which she sends UPS.

When it comes, I rush home and try it on. It fits perfectly. Mom, in all her good taste, has picked a dress that's simple but just a little daring. I model it in front of the mirror, pleased.

But something is missing.

I should be modeling this for Leecia. We should be giggling together and talking about what fun we'll have at the dance. The scene is so clear to me, I can almost taste it.

A feeling of emptiness begins in my stomach and then expands inside me, crowding out my lungs, my heart, squeezing a tear from my eye. Then another.

Leecia is in my life, but she's not. It's her presence here that makes the absence so sharply bitter. Everything in our suite — the tea kettle, the posters — reminds me of how things used to be. I can't help thinking, What if? What if? Where would we be now if this Professor T incident had never happened?

I can't just replace Leecia with Stacy. Things don't work that way. But how can I patch something that seems way beyond repair but is too painful to let go?

Tears begin to stain my face in earnest, but I don't bother to wipe them away.

There's a noise at the door. It opens, and Leecia comes in. She looks at me in her latest fashion: like I'm a piece of furniture, and she's just checking to see if I'm here. If she notices my misery, she doesn't show it. She is switched into her ignore-Ellen mode, walking about, putting her stuff away, getting ready to make a cup of tea.

"Leecia, I miss you," I say. It comes out as a kind of croak. Leecia doesn't turn her head, but there's no way she hasn't heard me. "I miss the way things were. Maybe we can't be real friends anymore, but can't we even talk? Share a cup of tea without staring at each other in anger? With all the things wrong in the world, it's so sad to maintain bad feelings between two people who used to be friends."

Leecia's lips twitch as if she might speak, but instead she

gathers up her tea and some books and goes into the bedroom.

I go to the common room closet, pull out our friendship quilt, and put it on the couch.

"Remember this quilt?" I say in the direction of the bedroom. "Remember the day we bought it? Our friendship quilt. And think of how much fun we had at the Head of the Charles."

There is a rustling from the bedroom — nothing extraordinary. I wipe my face, blow my nose, and take off the dress.

That night Jae and I go see *Sa-I-Gu*, a special documentary film about immigrant Korean women shopkeepers and how their lives were changed by the riots. *Sa-i-gu* is Korean for April 29; Koreans in L.A. largely refer to the riots this way. Almost all of the KASH people are here, but there are also some Alliance people and other non-Koreans.

The film starts with clips of overly familiar footage of burning stores, looters, armed Koreans. But then interspersed between these clips are stark sections of interviews with Korean women involved in the riots. All lost their stores; one lost a son.

There is one scene I remember from CNN: a mob of people gleefully carry armloads of clothes out of a dry cleaner's while a Korean woman pleads with them to stop, and three cops observe the scene with sickening casualness from across the street.

Jae's shoulders start to shake.

I had begun to believe that Jae never cried. But who could see this and not be touched? To him, it must be like watching a home movie of his worst memories.

"It's okay," I whisper to him in the dark, holding him, wiping his tears away.

When the movie ends, Jae wants to leave the auditorium quickly. He doesn't talk to anyone; he just keeps his head down.

"What if the riots had never happened?" he mumbles once we're outside. We're huddling close together as if we're cold, although the April night is warm.

"Things could be so different," he says. "My parents could be here. They wouldn't hate America. They would be with me."

"I wish they could be here," I say. I look up at the night sky. Black, with no stars.

Jae sighs. "Ellen, I'm tired of being strong. I'm tired of carrying this all the time. But what can I do? Quit work? Drop out of school? Go back to Korea? I just feel like whatever I do isn't going to make a hell of a difference at this point."

"So much of life is just about surviving, isn't it?" I laugh a cold, hollow laugh. "My father once talked about how leaving Korea was like being an animal that gnaws off its own leg to escape from a trap. You just have to go on with what you have."

"But that's just it," he says. "Being here at Harvard, you meet so many people who don't realize what they have. They've never had to work a day in their lives, they're given BMWs as high school graduation presents. Why is it that people like your parents and mine have had to start two steps back in the race? It's not fair."

"It's because we're minorities," I say. Then I add, "Like African Americans."

Jae looks startled for a moment. Then he folds his arms and nods, very slowly.

*

Maybe I'll write about all of this one day, I think as I lie in bed listening to Leecia breathing softly just a few feet away. But how would I explain it?

Every so often I forget that things are the way they are and I offer Leecia a cup of tea, or joke about something, and then Leecia looks at me as if to say, How on earth could you forget? Things are not the same.

And what exactly was it that changed everything, pulled us apart? We've argued before, disagreed before — what fun would friendship be if you agreed on everything all the time? I don't want to say it's because I'm Korean and she's black; maybe the people who saw us arguing on TV would think that way, but there's so much more to it. And if I could figure out exactly what went wrong and then fix it, I would.

But I think I'm coming to realize that life in all its complexity doesn't work like that. I could spend the rest of my life trying to figure out what went wrong, and I probably still wouldn't know.

Chapter Forty-One

"I'M READY to talk," Leecia says when I come back in from tae kwon do practice. There are two steaming cups of tea waiting, but her face is still the face of the new, unfamiliar Leecia.

"I hardly know where to begin," I say, sitting down.

"Why don't you start at the beginning — how you got involved with that Korean group."

I breathe in deeply, then exhale the entire tale: my trip to the music store, listening to the album, my change of heart.

"Why didn't you tell me about it, then?" Leecia says. "We used to tell each other everything."

"I guess I was afraid you'd change my mind," I say. "I wanted to stay mad at Professor T. I was mad at him about L.A., about what happened to families like Jae's and Sookie's — and how it could happen again."

"Mad enough that you'd betray me?"

"I didn't think of it as a betrayal. Maybe a sin of omission," I explain. "The people at KASH wanted a way to get their banner up, and switching it with the Alliance's was the perfect way. ~~Obviously, I couldn't tell you, or it~~ wouldn't work."

"Ellen, I can't believe you," Leecia says. "Did you ever stop to think about my feelings, our feelings at the Alliance? I personally had a lot riding on the welcoming rally. It took lots of work to get this guy to come here."

"I should have thought more about you," I say. "It was my mistake. But I guess I was also kind of surprised that you believe in that 'Get Down, Nuke Koreatown.' "

"I believe that Professor T has his points," Leecia says. "I don't want to get into all that right now. But really, we just wanted to bring a good entertainer, an African American, to campus for Spring Weekend. Who can fault us for that?"

"You seemed to have political motives too, judging from what you said to me at the rally."

"I was fired up, perhaps," Leecia says, not noticing the irony of her words. "And as I said, I don't want to get into that."

"Why not?" I ask. "How you feel about Koreans is important to me — I'm Korean."

"But you're not the same type as Jae and Sookie. Your dad's a doctor."

"So?" I say. "Our families have lots of things in common. Our parents all came to America hoping for a better life for their kids. They all want to make an honest living, help other people, and get their kids a good education — like your folks. Jae's family did employ an African American worker."

"I didn't know that," Leecia says.

"What else do you want to know?" I say.

Leecia shrugs.

We drink the rest of our tea in a silence that has recently become familiar. Things are never going to be like they were, I am beginning to realize. They can't be.

"I'm glad we had this talk," I say.

"Me too," Leecia agrees. The hardness in her eyes seems permanent, and I feel a tinge of sadness, knowing the part I had in putting it there.

*

Jae and I go to the formal. He is adorable in his vintage Keezer's tux.

Of course, we constantly run into Leecia. Irwin tried to make the space nice and intimate so we could be "one big happy dorm." But every time, even when Leecia and I are right next to each other at the punch bowl, we don't speak, other than one very brief hello at the beginning of the night. We pretend to be polite strangers, and we do it smoothly. It almost feels natural.

Almost.

Chapter Forty-Two

O N T H E D A Y that the weather in Cambridge turns seriously summery, I get a letter with an Arkin return address on it.

Holding my breath, I slowly tear it open.

"Is it from Jessie?" asks Jae, watching my face.

"It looks like her handwriting," I say.

"Want me to leave you alone to read it?" he asks.

"No, stay," I say, and I open it all the way so that he can read it too.

Unfolded, it is a single page.

> Ellen,
>
> I'm still very mad at you for what you did —
> you hurt me a lot. But I got to thinking, and I was
> remembering that time last summer when
> Marsha Randall bashed your face in with a bottle
> and for a moment I thought you were dead. With
> all the things we've gone through together, I realized that there shouldn't be anything we can't
> work out.

I still want you to be the maid of honor at my wedding. It'll be on October 27, just in time for Halloween (scary!). I do want you to be there. We can talk more this summer.

Jessie

Jae gently brushes my hair away from my face. "You see?" he says. "Things will get better."

I look at him. He's been there for me all this time, never wavering in his loyalty, always ready to listen to my problems.

"No," I say. "Things have always been good. I'm a very lucky person."

Despite the beautiful weather, Jae and I head into Widener. It's time to start studying for our finals.

Chapter Forty-Three

WHEN SUMMER VACATION ARRIVES, the time for Leecia and me to break up officially, each wants the other to have the friendship quilt.

"It's still a nice quilt," I say.

"It is," Leecia says. "But it's too heavy for me."

Too heavy with memories, I think.

"I'll return it to the store, then," I say. "Recycling."

"I'll go with you," Leecia declares.

"You don't have to," I say. "It's so far."

"That's why I'll go with you."

We end up going on the day Leecia's parents come to pick her up. We both trek through Cambridge, back into the neighborhood of the high school, the Korean deli. Some kids pass us, jabbering excitedly about their plans for the summer.

We donate the quilt, return home. Leecia's parents have arrived by then, and they greet me cordially.

"It's been fun," Leecia says, once all her stuff has been loaded into the U-Haul attached to the family's Volvo station wagon.